
★

"That body, or whatever, might have been deliberately buried and in resurfacing maybe the bones have shifted, too. But the position of the bones makes me think that body was kneeling when it died."

"A murder, then?"

"Or an execution."

"Wouldn't there be clothing or something to identify it as human?"

"Not in all that clay. It's acidic. Almost any fiber will dissolve in that soil in six years. If it's a murder, whoever did it is still here and dangerous."

★

"...a clever climax."

—*Publishers Weekly*

"Westfall pulls it all together..."

—*Kirkus Reviews*

Previously published by Worldwide Mystery by
PATRICIA TICHENOR WESTFALL

FOWL PLAY

PATRICIA TICHENOR WESTFALL

MOTHER OF THE BRIDE

W✺RLDWIDE.

TORONTO • NEW YORK • LONDON
AMSTERDAM • PARIS • SYDNEY • HAMBURG
STOCKHOLM • ATHENS • TOKYO • MILAN
MADRID • WARSAW • BUDAPEST • AUCKLAND

For my sisters, Nancy and Mary Jane

MOTHER OF THE BRIDE

A Worldwide Mystery/June 1999

First published by St. Martin's Press, Incorporated.

ISBN 0-373-26312-0

Visit us at www.worldwidemystery.com

Printed in U.S.A.

MOTHER
OF
THE
BRIDE

PART ONE

SOMETHING OLD

ONE

PHONE

ONE RING; two rings; five.

"Molly?"

"Mmph?"

"Molly, wake up. Get the phone."

"Mmph, you get it," she grumbled to her husband. Ken tried to reach over and through the mounds of goose-down comforters and quilts that were tangled over them both. The jumble of covers was ordinary February prudence made necessary by their living on a back-country road. Propane trucks took days to make deliveries if the roads were clear and did not deliver at all if roads were iced. Molly and Ken dared not run low on fuel in February, so they slept with the thermostat low and the blankets high. This made for some desperate nightly struggles. Both had mastered the art of the "delta clutch," or the ability to grab on to blankets even when in the deepest form of sleep—delta sleep—if the other turned over and threatened to take the covers along. Even so, their efforts to keep mutually covered created a fractured bed-scape every morning that rivaled the effects of colliding tectonic plates.

Ken could almost touch the phone on her bedside dresser but not quite. "Can't. You get it. You're closer."

Eight rings. Ten rings.

"All right. All right." She grabbed it. "The number you have reached is not in service, especially at"—she squinted at the glowing bedside clockface—"three a.m.? This had better be damned important."

"Hi, Molly, good morning to you, too."

"John?"

John Matins, as in Sheriff John Matins, as in next-door-neighbor Sheriff John Matins and his wife, Betty, although it was next door in a country sense, since their two houses were half a mile apart.

"Yes, the hardworking neighborhood sheriff, none other. Sorry to call so early, but I need Amanda's phone number." Amanda was Ken and Molly's twenty-five-year-old daughter, the elder of their two children.

"At three in the morning?"

"I'm sorry, yes. I need her help."

"Why? What's happened?" Molly was wide awake now. No matter how old children get, those mother-in-action hormones will surge into the bloodstream at the slightest threat to one.

"Luke Siever's escaped from prison. I've got a deputy guarding Bonnie's house right now, but I expect she's in terrible danger until he's caught again. I want her out of the Tricounty. Thought she could stay with Amanda in Cleveland, those two being such good friends'n all. Want Bonnie to start up driving now."

"But Amanda's coming home today. We're going to plan her wedding. You want to wait until she gets here or call her now anyway?"

"Wedding? Those two finally set a date? And you didn't tell us?"

"Oh. Been busy. Slipped my mind. Slipped entirely. Consider yourself told."

She heard him turn away from the phone. "Betty, wake up; Amanda's getting married."

Now Betty took the phone, her voice at once sleepy

and alert. "Bently and Amanda finally set a date? When?"

"April."

"So fast? Oh my dear Lord. Two months from now, that's going to be tricky, us getting things ready in two months. Well, we can do it, you and me. We'll have such fun, a wedding to plan. I love weddings. My Sherry's not yet give me one, so I'll make do with Amanda's. Who's doing the gown?"

She's joking, Molly half thought, half prayed. Please let her be babbling because she's sleepy. Betty is going to help and comfort me, not drive me crazy, right? I can't do this wedding thing. Everybody meddling, everybody bossing me.

In this rural southern part of Ohio, neighbors were more than nearby dwellers. They were like family. And like family they assumed Molly's business was theirs. Given the Appalachian heritage of the region, it wasn't particularly strange that both John and Betty would temporarily forget about some dangerous felon loose in the thick southern forests when there was something as exciting as a wedding to discuss. Hill folk had their priorities on straight.

"Uh, Betty, it *is* three in the morning," Molly said.

"When will she get here?" John had taken the phone back.

"Midafternoon. She said she'd start driving early."

"Maybe it'll be safe to wait about sending Bonnie away until she gets here. Even if Luke hitches rides, it'll take him some hours to get down here from Lima to us."

"Don't you think they'll recapture him soon? They'll have searchers out, won't they?"

"Yes, but Luke, I say he's part ghost. He can disappear

in a woods if he wants. Have Amanda call me the minute she gets here.''

"I will."

Ken had dropped back to sleep and was snoring lightly, but there was no more sleep for Molly. She lay awake thinking about that terrible day almost two years ago when Luke had beaten and shot his wife, Bonnie, then left her for dead in their trailer. Somehow, Bonnie had crawled to a phone and called the sheriff. Matins, in turn, had called in the helicopter that saved her life, first by stabilizing her at the scene and then by lifting her to a trauma center in Columbus.

When Amanda heard about the shooting she had come down from Cleveland to Columbus to keep vigil. The two women had been girlhood "best" friends. Molly had joined Amanda several times outside the intensive care unit to keep her company. Florence Wheeler, Bonnie's mother, and her aunt, Zenith Wheeler, also would come, and occasionally the four women were present at the same time, sitting on the uncomfortable vinyl chairs outside the hospital's trauma ward, mostly in silence, as Bonnie struggled to survive. The sight of Bonnie's pale form bristling with tubes still haunted Molly.

Bonnie had been the first to befriend then ten-year-old Amanda when the family had moved down from Chicago for Ken's new job as a professor at the college. Most of the kids in school teased Amanda at first. She dressed funny and talked extremely funny. Appalachian kids thought her Chicago "dese" and "dose" were hilarious. Bonnie was also an outcast because she was from a troubled family. Every region has a few such families, and the Wheelers were the Tricounty version. As a newcomer, Molly didn't know to warn Amanda away from the Wheelers. Amanda's social skills soon meant Bonnie had new friends, too, whether their mothers approved or not. But Bonnie and Amanda were always best friends.

Amanda had loved playing at Bonnie's house because of its secret places. There were crawl spaces under the stairs and closets behind the closets. There were secret panels in the attic and hidden hallways within the walls. The house, a decaying antebellum structure of Italianate style, sat on a bluff overlooking the Ohio River. It had been built by Clement Barton, a river pirate who became wealthy in the surge of river commerce that followed the building of the Baltimore & Ohio Railroad through present-day West Virginia in the 1830s and 1840s. At one time, Riverport, the town beneath the Mansion's bluff, rivaled Cincinnati in cachet and wealth. Now it was a mere spot on the map, gone except for weed-infested foundations and a few brick chimneys standing like tombstones amid the brush.

In the heady years before the Civil War, when water transport was opening the West, the Bartons, with help from an occasional bribe and a murder or two, were one of the most powerful families in southern Ohio. The next generation of Bartons had been abolitionists, and the Mansion became renowned as a station on the Underground Railroad. Clement Barton, Jr., and his wife Esmerelda funneled hundreds of escapees northward toward ports on Lake Erie where they could get passage to Canada. It was risky work because, under the Fugitive Slave Act, anyone caught harboring slaves or assisting runaways would forfeit their property. Every bounty hunter knew the Barton Mansion housed runaways, but so clever was the series of caves and tunnels behind and under the house and so well designed was the system of bells to warn fugitives of danger that none was recaptured from the Barton house despite almost nightly raids. The same system of bells and caves greatly enriched a later Barton during Prohibition.

Florence Barton Wheeler, Bonnie's mother, had inherited the house when her own mother died and she moved into it with David, her husband, when Bonnie was two. Six years ago and a year after Bonnie's own marriage, David had left Florence for parts unknown. No one had seen or heard from him since. Florence should have been relieved since David was "a hitter," the term locals used to describe wife beaters. Florence, however, was deeply hurt by the abandonment. She told anyone and everyone she wanted him to come home and get down on his knees begging for her forgiveness. That's all she wanted, she'd say, for her husband to beg.

David Wheeler had also routinely beaten Bonnie, a fact Amanda knew but didn't tell her mother until she was grown. Bonnie often went to school dirty or bruised from a beating in those days. The two girls learned to use the Mansion's hiding places whenever David was home.

As a teenager, Amanda became fascinated with the notorious house and its family. She loved to imagine she was Esmerelda Barton, feeding soup to hungry, frightened runaways, shushing their fears, and putting salve on their whip welts. Bonnie was often her "runaway," Amanda tending her all-too-real welts. The girls put cots in one of the caves and stocked it with canned goods and first-aid supplies. Their tunnel was snug and dry, an ideal place to weather David's rages. They kept their cache a secret from Florence, too. Both were sure she would tell David if she knew.

The house became for Amanda a place to sort out her own adolescence. Amanda was a bewildered teen because she was basically a social child who couldn't abide social organizations. She had hated Girl Scouts because the troop leader was a stunted woman who thought it more important for young girls to wear gloves and make beds with crisp hospital corners than to go hiking. A muddy girl was an abomination, in this woman's view. Amanda was for mud and messy beds and against gloves. She quit Scouts. She'd also tried 4-H, had loved raising the animals, but hated the club's business emphasis on selling animals for meat at the end of the fair season. To Amanda that was criminal. How could anyone eat a goat, especially one as sweet as her Nubian, Daisy, or the kids, Frank and Jethro? She washed out of 4-H.

Then in high school she discovered Civil War history and, with the help of a local historical society, started a women's Civil War reenactor's group which they named the Damn Yankees Club. Bonnie, who did everything Amanda did, joined, of course, and the girls marched in many a Labor Day and Fourth of July parade in their hoopskirts. Amanda recruited women and teens from West Virginia, Kentucky, and southern Ohio for her club. She even persuaded Florence to let the group host Victorian teas at the Mansion a few times. As Amanda and Bonnie became more serious about the hobby, both became sticklers for accuracy. Bonnie was especially serious, as if she needed the club for something more than friendship and role-playing. She became the club's custodian of the proof book, a scrapbook they kept to document the accuracy of their dress and deportment.

Amanda and Bonnie's Civil War hobby held together a friendship that might otherwise have withered because the two women were certain to have different destinies. Bonnie, limited by her abusive childhood, escaped into an early, disastrous marriage. Her only career skill was an ability with makeup; she worked as cosmetics consultant for the department store in town. Amanda, the privileged child of a loving and educated family, went to the Cleveland Institute of Art, earned a bachelor's in graphic design, landed a good job with a publishing company, had been promoted twice and, oh yes, met Bently Cottingham of *the* Cleveland Cottinghams, as in the very wealthy Cleveland Cottinghams. Bonnie and Amanda might no longer have had anything in common if it weren't for the Civil War or the Barton Mansion. But so intense was that one link, Amanda wanted Bonnie to be her matron of honor.

Amanda had told her mother a few things about Bonnie's troubled childhood during those long vigils in the hospital hall. Molly had never known the girl was abused, or, she had thought ruefully at the time, she might not have let Amanda play with Bonnie either. How could she not have known? she rebuked herself.

Betty Matins had tried to reassure her friend. "Country distances are so big," she'd said. "I'm your closest neighbor but still half a mile away. The Barton Mansion is twenty miles away. How could you know what goes on in a home twenty miles away?" The Wests' home was fifteen miles north of the Tricounty's one and only town, New Forge; the Barton Mansion five miles south of the town. All Tricounty children were bused into the schools in New Forge every day. Whenever Amanda wanted to spend the night with Bonnie, she'd take an overnight bag and ride Bonnie's bus after school. When Bonnie stayed at the Wests', she'd ride Amanda's bus. So in all the years the girls had been friends, Molly had needed to visit the Barton Mansion only a handful of times. During that time, Amanda never told her about the beatings or the many nights the girls had hidden from David. It was their secret.

Betty's sympathy had no effect. How could a mother have been so unaware? Molly could not be comforted. Her husband Ken, a sociology professor, tried to reassure her, too.

"Rarely do violent men seem disturbed to outsiders. In fact, the opposite; they can be quite charming, extroverted even. You can't blame yourself for not seeing it," he'd said.

"But why didn't Amanda tell us?"

"And what would you have done?"

"Not let Amanda go over there."

"Right, and thus have taken from Bonnie the one source of support she had."

"But Amanda could have been in danger."

"Also true. What is the right thing to do about family violence, eh?"

As Bonnie recovered, Amanda and Sheriff Matins entreated her to testify against Luke. They didn't need her testimony to launch a case, but they needed it to defuse a possible defense of "accidental shooting," Matins explained.

"He's dangerous, Bonnie. For your sake and for his, he must go to prison," Amanda had argued.

Her mother, Florence, was opposed. "Not right for a woman to speak against her husband. He'll get you eventually. He'll get his revenge," she'd said.

In the end Bonnie agreed to testify and Luke was given a twenty-year sentence. It had been eighteen months since he had been sent upstate to the medium-security prison in Lima. Now he was loose, probably seeking revenge, just as Florence had predicted. Molly shuddered.

TWO

DESK

MOLLY WENT early to her office, if a corner with a sec-
ondhand desk in a classroom of a former elementary
school in town could be called an "office." The windows
beside her desk were ten feet tall, spilling abundant light
over her chaos of papers. Molly, by training, was an accountant, but by temperament, she was an engineer of
disorder, able to create a splendid disarray with a mini-
mum of materials. Her house was a monument to clutter,
her desk a triumph of sedimentary layering. For Christmas one year her son, Todd, had given her an ornately
framed calligraphy text that said, "A tidy desk is the
province of a sick mind." The text occupied a position
of honor on her desk, between a photo of her family and
another of her dog, Goldie, but all three frames were half-
obscured by a stack of client records she was pretending
to update. In actuality, however, she was fretting.

As she had started to leave the house earlier, Ken had
called to her from his study to come look. He was surfing
the World Wide Web, as he did every morning, and had
just come across Luke's picture on "Ohio's Most
Wanted" home page. Molly stood behind Ken's chair,
watching the site's pixels slowly resolve into a sharp im-
age of Luke's bony face, with its intense blue eyes. His
hair was straight and unruly. In the profile shot beside it,
his chin jutted forward, intensifying the hollows of his
cheeks. Molly felt a chill of pure horror as she gazed into

those digital eyes. During the drive into New Forge, the radio station led its newscast with the story of his escape. "Was he armed?" a reporter asked. They didn't know, the prison spokeswoman said. "Was he dangerous?" another asked. Any escaped felon was considered dangerous, she'd said.

Molly's husband taught rural culture and criminal behavior in his sociology courses, so she knew from him that the notion rural areas were somehow safer than urban was illusion. Ken could produce statistics and studies to prove that on a per capita basis rural crime was higher than urban crime. But numbers, per capita or otherwise, did not carry the impact of those computerized eyes staring at her with such menace. The Internet made our dangerous times too understandable, she thought. Then she silently scolded herself: Shake free of it. Get to work.

For a few minutes she did just that, buried herself in the gentler troubles and concerns of the Tricounty Meal Van Service. She had been associate director of this agency for fourteen of the fifteen years the couple had lived in southern Ohio. She'd had to leave a promising career in a Chicago bank when Ken was offered his position at Sycamore State College in New Forge. But since the Meal Van work was so satisfying, she'd never felt any regrets. Together, she and the director, Patsy Bonneau, had built the service from the back of Patsy's station wagon into a fleet of six specially equipped catering trucks delivering more than ninety hot lunches to seniors and shut-ins every weekday. Just last month they had started a walk-in meal service by converting one of the classrooms into a dining room. Already about twenty elderly were coming by each noon.

Her duties as associate director were a little bit of everything, from changing the oil in the vans to scrubbing pots, but in theory her job was supposed to be managing the Meal Van's budget and revenues. Worrying about finding the money to keep it all going sometimes kept her awake nights. The Meal Van asked its clients to pay what they could, but few could afford to pay the full value of the meals. The chronic shortage of cash stretched her business skills to the limit. What sustained her was the certain knowledge that the service meant that scores of families could keep elderly loved ones at home, and scores more of elderly living alone got at least one hot meal a day. Banking had never given her that kind of satisfaction, the knowledge that she was making a real difference in people's lives.

She had managed to date and record fees received from about twenty clients when her mind began to wander off again, this time to Amanda and Bonnie, until she brought herself up short again. I'll make a list, she thought. Maybe that will help me concentrate.

In this, at least, she and her daughter were alike. There were times Molly felt as if lists were the only thing the two had in common anymore. Amanda was as dedicated a listmaker as her mother, and she had once rebuked her father for teasing them about their lists. Amanda had told him a good list was a work of art. Like art, it had form and meaning, order and idea. "Like art, a list evokes reality by means of dream," she'd said.

"Dream?" Molly asked, wondering suddenly how any child of hers could be so didactic.

"Yes, dream. Have you ever finished the tasks on any list?"

"No."

"A list, then, is the world as you imagine it to be, not as it is."

Molly was confused. "If a list is imagination, how can it be reality?" she'd asked.

"Isn't imagination the supreme reality?" Amanda had replied.

It was all too deep for a mere accountant, Molly had decided, and let the subject drop, but for a while she had saved her lists. Who knew, they might be artworks of value. A week ago, when Amanda had called to tell her parents that she and Bently had finally set a date, she'd had a detailed list at hand, of course. She would get home from Cleveland on Friday, she'd said. They would plan the wedding then, but in the meantime would Molly talk to a bridal planner.

A bridal planner indeed, as if there were a choice in rural southern Ohio. *The* bridal planner, the only one for six counties around, was Zenith Shield Wheeler, Bonnie's aunt. The week had slipped away to become today and Molly had not yet visited Zenith, so intense was her dread. Was it the wedding she dreaded, or the two months that she would have to work closely with Amanda? The daughter had slight patience with the mother. The two had not had a conversation in thirteen years that had not ended in a fuss. Amanda had begun sassing at age twelve and now at twenty-five was still, always, and predictably, snappish to her mother.

"Mother, we want a big wedding, just everybody we know there. And all my best friends as bridesmaids," she'd said when she'd called.

"How many best friends do you have, dear?" Molly had asked.

"Ten. There's Dawn, Sherry, Lorraine, Connie, Amy, Jennifer, Mary—" Of course there was a Jennifer. There was always a Jennifer or two in any group of twenty-year-olds.

"Ten? Amanda, there won't be room in the church for guests."

"And Bonnie—Bonnie's to be matron of honor—and—"

"Amanda, I'm not sure your father and I can afford—"

"Mother, is that how you think of me? As an expense?" Amanda had replied, and then started to cry.

Molly usually ignored such tears since Amanda could cry at anything, even a sentimental television commercial. But two months of these scenes? How would she stand it?

"No, dear, I want you to have the best wedding possible, but we have to be reasonable."

"We'll use our own dresses, Mother, and handpick plain garden flowers."

"We have so much to talk about, dear—the invitations, the reception—"

"Let's serve peanut butter and jelly sandwiches. Think we can afford that?"

"Amanda, let's not quarrel. I'm sure that—"

And so on. Two months of this to go. And at the end, her least favorite of human activities, a wedding. Molly had never in her life enjoyed a wedding, not even, or maybe especially, her own. In-laws glaring, ushers drunk, children whining, music loud, food cold, makeup smudged, reception halls hot, toasts clumsy, the make-them-kiss routine silly, and the cake too, too icky sweet.

Obviously even a list wouldn't pull her out of her cranky train of thought. She tried work again, and began reviewing the purchase requisitions from their cook, who coincidentally, and thanks to Molly, was Betty Matins, and who, coincidentally, was walking in at the moment with a large paper grocery sack. She was smiling brightly—not unusual, that. Betty was one of life's relentless cheerful types. A tiny woman, plumpish, sweet-faced, with sun-weathered skin, she was slightly older than Molly's fifty-two, and was, as is traditional in hill country, a dedicated blonde for as long as blonde could be found in a bottle. She started to spill the contents of the sack onto Molly's desk.

"No, no don't," Molly protested, expecting cabbages, but what slid out in slick, glittering display instead were bridal magazines.

"Oh no. Worse than cabbages," Molly groaned.

"Look at this." Betty had already tabbed pages with a medley of color stick-on slips, pink, blue, green, yellow.

"When did you get up this morning?"

"Oh, I couldn't go back to sleep. I was so excited. I love weddings. I got right up and started marking magazines."

"You had these at home?"

Betty nodded vigorously. "I buy them all the time."

Now Molly knew she had died and gone to hell. Who was this stranger? She had known Betty for fifteen years. Theirs was the kind of friendship that traded sorrows, joys, and recipes. There could be no surprises between them anymore. And yet here she was, surprised. Now she felt bad for not telling Betty about the wedding sooner. She'd been denying her friend a real pleasure because of her own selfish dread of the thing.

Betty didn't seem to have noticed Molly's moodiness, or maybe she dismissed it as lack of coffee. That was how most people explained Molly's chronic morning grumpiness. Most times they were right, but this morning it was also lack of sleep and dread, dread, dread of the coming weekend.

"Betty, I have to talk to Zenith Wheeler later today for Amanda. You want to come?"

She beamed her assent.

"After I finish my run?" Molly had to drive one of the Meal Van routes that whole week because the regular driver's daughter was having a baby in Indianapolis. Molly smiled to herself, her mood lifting a bit. I'm becoming a true native, aren't I? she thought. A Chicagoan would have thought "because the driver had the week off." But, no, an Appalachian includes—even in her thoughts—not only where the woman had gone and why, but how things went (fine) and what the results were (boy, seven pounds eight ounces, name, Jeremy Michael).

THREE

HOOK

"SO SEVEN POUNDS, eight ounces? Tha's a good weight. Not too big, not too small." Louella Chalmers Benton, of course, already knew about Jeremy Michael. And she knew about Luke Siever, too. What Louella didn't know hadn't happened yet. She was the old lady no one ever surprised. As a former county commissioner, she knew everybody and everything, and knew it every which way from Sunday, as she liked to brag. This had made her useful to Sheriff Matins more than once.

Molly sat on a sofa struggling with the half double crochet stitch as Louella ate her lunch. Louella's was always the last stop on this Meal Van route, partly because the house was so remote, but partly because Molly liked to sit a while for her crochet lesson without keeping anybody else waiting for their meal. Molly had just told Louella about Amanda's peanut butter and jelly remark, to the older woman's delight. Louella considered obnoxiousness a talent and loved to hear about really good sass.

"No, no," Louella said, "tension's too tight. Yer pullin' through three loops wi' the ha'double. So keep it loose like. Looser. Looser. Good."

Molly frowned in concentration. Delivering the meal to Louella last meant she arrived well after one o'clock, by which time Louella was really hungry and consequently really cranky.

"Yer late," she had greeted Molly when the van pulled in to the yard.

"No I'm not. I never set a time," Molly shot back. She assembled Louella's meal with frowning fury from the back of the van. With rote motions from long experience, she took food first from the cold unit, next from the hot unit, then checked the temperatures with the probe. Louella waited with an even more furious frown on the porch. The seventyish native, partly crippled with arthritis, leaned on a cane that was almost as tall as she was. She wore a crocheted afghan as a shawl over a too-long print dress.

"I never said what time," Molly repeated defiantly, but truth was she was much later than usual, and it was February's fault. February was in full frost heave, an event of geological proportions in these southern hills of Ohio. Well, actually, it was a geological event, period. Moisture seeps between the horizontal layers of impermeable yellow clay throughout the hills forced water to leach out over cliff fronts. As the water dripped, it froze into spectacular icicles, some a hundred feet long, or more. Tourists from four states around came to see the icicles. Farther north it was too cold for seeps and farther south it was too warm for them to freeze, so the ice was unique to the region.

The tourists saw these ice displays only in the state parks, but there were many just as awesome on the back roads Molly drove. Icicles cascaded with heart-stopping beauty from ledge tops above these roads, but they also often broke or dripped. In the process they calved boulders loose from the cliffs or gouged potholes. The phenomenon made the poorly drained gravel a challenge even for Molly's four-wheel-drive van. It had been slow going from house to house that day.

Just walking with the meal trays from the van to the houses was difficult in frost-heave season. No one in the country had sidewalks, so Molly had to trudge through mud. She wore her farm-chore boots, but still the short hike from car door to house door was relentlessly sticky. On cloudy, moist days like this the frost heave actually made noise, a saturated squish, a continuous soft static sounding everywhere there was clay. It sounded in her yard. It sounded here in Louella's as she assembled the tray. Its hiss was gentle, oddly soothing, even if it also harbingered mud- and rockslides—so unlike the Chicago of her youth, where the ground lay quiet for all of February. Here the winter was restless, tossing up flower bulbs from their beds, rearranging rocks in rock gardens, redesigning bumps on paved roads.

But whenever she became weary of the mess that is February, she would turn into a hollow and chance on an example of its gift, the ice, as she had now at sight of a huge display that decked the bluff behind Louella's. She had watched this ice grow all week, and now it tiered like a pipe organ. The day's muted light made the milky blue icicles shimmer as if they were about to sound a cantata. Her eyes traveled the rippled ice from the ledge top down, down to the dripping points, down to the tiny house beneath them, down to Louella herself, scowling on the porch.

"I think you should be more punctual like," Louella complained. "You prob'ly ware late t'yer own wedding."

"Please don't mention weddings to me, Louella. Please don't."

Louella had raised a shocked eyebrow at that. Not like Molly to be sensitive. Insults were the Appalachian hello.

Louella herself had taught Molly how to greet people
properly. Taking offense was not proper at all.

"You feelin' poorly?" Louella said, genuinely concerned.

"I'm okay."

Louella had held the door, then followed Molly in,
thumping her cane heavily behind her. "Coffee's on the
stove, stuff's out ready for today's crochet lesson," she'd
said. Their bargain was that Louella would teach Molly
the skill and Molly would take Louella on occasional car
trips. Thus far, Louella had taught her the single, double,
and treble stitches and was now teaching her the half
double and some openwork stitches. Openwork was
much easier than the basic stitches, Molly had remarked.
Louella's reply had been that of course empty holes
would be easier than stitches.

Molly was ordinarily so eager for each day's lesson
that Louella was alarmed when Molly said she wouldn't
stay.

"Now I know something's wrong. You sit down right
this minit and tell me whut, y'hear?"

"No, Louella, I don't feel like talking just now."

"You don't talk, I don't eat."

Molly had laughed. "You can threaten with the best
of them, can't you? Maybe you're right, a little crochet
would make me feel better."

So she had sat down, taken up her work, and waited
for the silence to break. Part of Molly was still grumpy,
but another part of her was now curious about how this
reversal of roles was going to work. Usually it was Molly
pumping Louella for information and usually failing to
get any. Louella was the Tricounty know-it-all in part
because she could keep her mouth shut. She didn't tell

just anyone what she knew. With Louella now become the inquisitor, how would the conversation unfold?

Louella sipped her coffee. Finally she said, "Tension's too tight agin, dear, loosen the left-hand thread. No, now tha's too loose."

Silence again. Is this her technique? Molly thought. Dead silence until you crack?

Louella picked up her own crochet. "Too bad 'bout Bonnie," she said. "That girl never gets it easy, do she?"

Of course; a deflection strategy. I knew it, Molly thought. "That whole family is troubled, isn't it?" Molly said. I'm going to make her work for this, she thought. I'll not give her one sentence without a struggle.

"Yes, a very troubled clan," Louella said.

"I don't know much about the Wheelers. Have they been in the Tricounty long?" Molly said.

"I warn't thinking 'bout the Wheelers, though they's bad enough."

"The Bartons?"

"Yes, there's a family tha's more than peculiar. One generation they's saints, the next they's sinners, never in the middle."

"Really?"

"First generation was a river brigand, that's the Clement whut built that mansion. Next Clement was a Presbyterian minister and an abolitionist, probably saved hundreds of runaways' lives. But his son, Clement III, prob'ly kilt as many as Clement II saved because conditions in his iron mines and foundries ware so poor. The next Clement helped start the college in town."

"Sycamore State? My husband's college?"

"Of course yer husband's college. Whut other college is there?"

"Then was the next Barton a sinner?"

"A big-time bootlegger. Then the next Clement, the last one, Florence's father, ware a good man. He began that department store in New Forge, though he lost it all agin in Jimmy Carter's recession. Went bankrupt, had to sell, poor man."

"The store where Bonnie works now?"

"Yes, but ain't Luke's upset you," Louella stated.

"Well he has, but that's not the only thing. I'd hoped to have more time before Amanda married. I wanted to crochet her a veil, and now, with the wedding only two months away, there's no way I could have enough squares done by April. Why does she want to get married so quickly?" Molly said.

Louella laughed. "Why you silly. Cain't you guess? A gran'chil's on the way. Lot o'gals in these parts marry in a hurry."

"I don't think so. Amanda's totally modern. I can't imagine her letting herself get pregnant with her career so important to her. And even if she was, she wouldn't be embarrassed by it and keep it from us; she'd instead want to tell us the good news. No, the rush to get married is because something else is going on."

"And you don't know?"

"Haven't a clue."

"Scary when our children become strangers, ain't it?" Louella stretched her work to balance the stitches.

"Is that it? Is it me? Is it her wedding means I've lost her? She's not my little girl anymore?"

"Thar's a hill saying hereabouts. 'Yer son is yer son 'til he marries. Yer daughter is yer daughter forever.' I only had boys, so I don't know 'bout that last."

"It's a comforting thought. What I can't figure, though, is why I'm so upset all the time. How hard can it be to plan a wedding? Yet I'm grouchy, and I start crying at odd times. This isn't like me at all. I can't even make lists."

Louella sat up at that. She, too, was a member of the world's cadre of listmakers. She knew it was serious when a listmaker didn't feel like making lists. She leaned forward in her chair, and, with uncharacteristic gentleness, said, "Molly? Have you been through the Change yet?"

Molly choked, both shocked and bemused by the question and equally bemused to realize she had given in to Louella's understated questioning with barely a struggle. She was trying to think what to say when both women heard a car, then saw a sheriff's cruiser squishing into the mud in front. Matins got out of it, slowly uncurling himself, grimacing, annoyed by the way close-to-the-road vehicles like the cruiser forced his limbs to tangle. He much preferred his high-riding pickup. He also preferred his farm clothes to a sheriff's uniform and today had compromised by enduring the regulation blue shirt and the regulation tool belt with its dangling law-officer paraphernalia—gun, beeper, keys, whatever. But his other clothes were regulation farm store: jeans, John Deere hat, boots, ragg wool socks. Over the sheriff shirt he had put on an oversize plaid flannel shirt, which he wore unbuttoned like a jacket. His clothes plus his height and extreme thinness made him look country to the core, which in fact he was. He smiled as he spied the women through the window. The smile transformed him. His weathered face, seamed from years of farming, hunting, and fishing, reforged into gentle wrinkles. That smile, Betty always said, was better protection than a gun; it could soothe the churliest drunk.

Matins pretend banged at the door, pretend hollered,

"Louella, you decent?" and barged in. "Hi, Molly," he said. "How'd you sleep last night?"

"Damn little, thanks to you," she growled appropriately. Native etiquette demanded an insult on first greeting.

"I had the weirdest dream after I hung up from you," he said, settling on the edge of one of Louella's cloth-draped armchairs. "I dreamed I was sleep deprived. Weird to be sleeping and sleep deprived at the same time."

He looked sleep deprived, Molly thought. "I had a crazy dream, too," she said. "I dreamed the new 911 service put me on hold."

He laughed. "That's already happened. Martha Sherwin, she does 911 three nights a week. She got flustered on her first call and hit hold. Penny Lopez's husband was having chest pains, and she's put on hold, poor woman."

"I hadn't heard that. Did he die?" Louella said.

"Nah, he's okay, but I've got to find time to train everyone some more. I've got to have more real staff. This trying to police an area this big with part-timers and volunteers isn't working, obviously."

"Obviously? Why 'obviously'?" Molly said.

His face turned serious. "Well, obviously for the reason I came to see Louella, and I was planning *only* on speaking to Louella, but I'm just too polite a guy to throw out her company, so, Molly, if you want to stay, you're an official volunteer. Sure you want the responsibility?"

"Well, because of Amanda, aren't I involved already?"

"What?"

"You know, because of Luke."

"Oh, that. No. Last night I thought Luke was the biggest damn problem on the planet. But this morning comes a bigger problem.''

"Bigger?''

"Like I said, if I include you, then you're official. Sure you two want to be official semitemporary deputies?''

Molly exchanged glances with Louella. Both women shrugged.

"Okay, then I want you two to take the official semitemporary oath.''

"Lordy, John,'' Louella snapped. "You been here seventeen jillion times and you never made this much fuss. Get on with it.''

"The oath. I insist.''

Louella handed him her Bible.

"Molly, do you swear to the best of your ability to carry out such duties as you are charged with and to keep confidential all matters under investigation until such time as I release you from duty?''

"How long is this duty going to last before I swear to that?''

"It's only one investigation I'm swearing you in for.''

"Okay, then I do.''

"Louella, do you swear to ditto?''

"Johnny, you orter get more sleep, y'hear? Yer actin' goofy.''

"I'll take that as an 'I do.' Okay, now remember you're secret deputies, especially you Louella, since you talk to everybody. And you, Molly, are you going to be driving for the Meal Van anytime soon?''

"All next week.''

"Think you can contrive for some driving most every week for a while?''

"Easily.''

"Good. We've got big trouble in the Tricounty. I get

to the office this morning to find a half dozen FBI and ATF waiting.''

"Luke's that dangerous?''

"Nah. They ain't interested in silly old Luke. They think we've got a gun smuggler set up here, maybe even a paramilitary group.''

"Like those crazies in Montana?''

"More specifically like those crazies in Arizona. One of their informants says guns have been shipped from Arizona to this area. Don't know to whom and don't know what's happened to them after that, but they're serious guns, semiautomatics, could be converted to full automatics. Could be the Arizona group suspected they'd been compromised and hurried to pass the torch to another group here.''

"Is that the group they caught with all those guns and floor plans to federal offices?''

"I think so, yeah. So maybe we got a branch of that group here or maybe we got a local contraband dealer. Either way, I want them out of my county, that's fer sure.''

"Couldn't it be both, smuggling and a group?'' Molly said.

"Why do you think that?''

"Ever since I've lived here I've noticed how most people have to have two sources of income, like Formby has his hardware store and funeral home or Allen Weinstein has an electrical service and goat dairy or Billy Ray Sweet does septic tank pumping and landscape service. I don't like to think too much about that last blend.''

"Zenith Wheeler, she has three,'' Louella added, "a tree nursery, a herbal tea business, and a bridal boutique.''

"Couldn't somebody be doing both, running a paramilitary group and selling guns on the side? Be more typical of people here," Molly continued.

"Interesting thought. A possibility, yes," John said. "Anyway, what I want you two to do is just listen. Any women complain about their husbands being gone too much, I want to know. Any men with overly muddy boots and it not be hunting season, I want to know. Anyone mention they heard some good ol' boys out target shooting in the woods, I want to know."

"I hear that all the time," Molly said.

"Well, listen real good for now."

"Why us?"

"Because I don't know much about these groups, but them FBI fellows gave me an earful of psychological profiles and such, and I'm thinking from them that these militarists are the kind of men who ignore their women. My guess is if I can plug into women's chat lines, I'll learn something because the men won't think to be cautious around women, women being no threat and all. You need to ply friends, Louella, but be discreet. If those women suspect what you're after, they'll start protecting their husbands and sons, and we'll get nowhere."

Molly looked at Louella and was shocked to see that her face was ashen and her hands trembled in her lap. "How do you feel about this, Louella?" she asked. "If there is a group here, chances are somebody mixed up in it will be related to a friend of yours."

"Might be related to me even."

"Maybe so, you got enough relations hereabouts," Matins said.

"I got to think on this. Could be this group are just kids at cowboy'n'Indians in the woods with sycamores the Indians."

"And it could be we got a real serious threat here, too.

Okay, you think. I'll talk to you some more later," Matins said.

"John, maybe I should tell Ken about this, too," Molly added. He's probably got some useful material stashed away in his criminology course files or knows some good Internet sites. He might be able to tell us something useful."

"That he would; okay, but you tell him, and I'll tell him myself later, secrecy. Be secret. These people are supposed to be mighty dangerous, the FBI thinks. I think the FBI can get all revved over nothing more dangerous than a tree full of bobcats. But for now, I'm gonna believe them. So keep mum. Okay, I've got to go, I'm late six to a million ways. Molly, I'll stop by and see Amanda and Dr. K later today." Dr. K was a student nickname for Ken.

Matins left, and the two women sat silently for a few minutes. Louella sipped her coffee. Molly hooked stitches.

"You know something already, don't you?" Molly said to Louella.

"Mebbe."

"Want to talk about it?"

"How are we going to get a veil ready in time for Amanda's wedding and her getting married so quick?" Louella said.

Whoa, she's really upset to change the subject that much, Molly thought, but she played along. "I guess the veil is not to be," she said. "It really hurts—I wanted to surprise her with a handmade veil, but even with you helping, it can't be done in two months."

"But with maybe a dozen ladies helping?"

Molly looked at her, baffled.

"I think it's time for a meeting of the Tricounty Old

Lady Network. Do you think the Meal Van might help with food and transportation?''

Molly smiled. ''John will be glad to hear of this.''

''Don't you tell him. Don't you ever tell him how I work.''

''Yes'm,'' Molly said.

''Tension's too tight agin; loosen up that left-hand thread.''

''Yes'm,'' Molly said again.

FOUR

TEA

MOLLY WEST, Betty Matins, and Zenith Shield Wheeler sat in Zenith's office discussing Bonnie Wheeler Siever's bust. Bonnie's bust was a huge problem, literally. It bunched sizably between neck and waistline, obscuring both, making Bonnie appear likely to tip over at any moment. How, Molly thought miserably as she struggled yet again to think of a fresh euphemism, does one do this? I don't know how to plan a wedding. I don't know how to be a mother of the bride, especially if it means I have to spend all my time discussing the physical shortcomings of Amanda's friends.

The office of Zenith's Bridal Boutique was, like everything else in the Tricounty, not quite what Molly had expected. It was a catalog-laden bench in a potting shed behind Zenith's greenhouse. To get to it, they had walked past long tables in the greenhouse, where teenagers were repotting flats of petunias, impatiens, salvia, and snapdragons. Practically every teenager in the Tricounty worked for Zenith in February to get bedding plants ready for May sales. Bonnie and Amanda had done that. So had Todd.

The three women sat in the cramped shed looking at pictures of satin gowns and lace veils while surrounded by bins of soil mix, vermiculite, and peat. Shelves of brightly colored plastic pots ringed the room over their heads. If the women saw a picture that interested them,

Zenith laid a trowel on the book to mark the page. The chairs for the consultation were three comfortable rockers, but the cushions were covered in plastic to protect them from the dust of the soil mixes.

According to Louella, Shield's Nursery had been in the Shield family for three generations. It grew dogwoods, redbuds, lilacs, and rhododendrons in fields south of the greenhouses. The nursery's main specialty, however, was wildflowers. Zenith's woods grew enough to supply a national garden mail-order company with hardy cyclamen, joe-pye weed, lily of the valley and goatsbeard. Zenith also harvested both wild and garden herbs to make a small quantity of packaged herbal teas which Breyers Mill then sold for her. Zenith not only knew which herbs were safe to drink, but also which weren't. She was fascinated by poisonous plants. The agricultural extension knew it could rely on her for advice about natural pesticides, and her recipe for dog flea dip was much treasured throughout the Tricounty.

She was a woman with no illusions, made so by a hard life. She was bony, her skin wrinkled from years of outdoor work. The nails of her hands were snagged from scrabbling in nursery beds. Her curly graying hair and pale eyes suggested that she might once have been pretty. Now, she just seemed nervous, her hands always in motion, often reaching for an omnipresent cup of herbal tea.

Zenith's husband, Robert, was useless. Both Wheeler boys were. Zenith's father had almost disinherited her when she'd married Robert Wheeler. A condition of his will had been that Zenith must keep sole ownership of the nursery, a provision she'd often quietly thanked him for when—long after her father died—she decided he had been right. At least, she had comforted herself over the years, she hadn't married the other one, David, who was just as lazy as Robert, but violent as well. Robert only hit Zenith occasionally.

To supplement the nursery income, which was seasonal at best, Zenith ran this bridal-planning service. As the only bridal planner in the Tricounty, she knew the couture needs of all its potential brides and bridesmaids. It was she who had brought up the problem of Bonnie's oversize bust.

"So maybe a bloused effect for the dress? To hide the bust?" Betty suggested.

"Oh no," Zenith said. "Think of Dolly Parton. She never wears baggy things, always tight, especially at the waist. And wide-open necklines. She hides her bust by calling attention to her waist and neck."

"I thought the necklines were to show cleavage," Molly said.

"Well, yes, but also to give the eye something other than those boobs to look at."

"But what about the other girls?" Betty said. "They'd look like fence posts in a dress like that."

"We'll modify the design." Zenith was already sketching.

"I think the girls want to make the dresses themselves," Molly said.

"Oh."

A pained silence.

"Um. Maybe we'd better talk about money first," Molly said.

"I thought a professor's wife…"

"Would you like to see our tax returns?" Molly snarled, surprised by her own anger.

"Oh, I'm so sorry, Molly." Zenith's apology was genuine. "I didn't mean to insult you. Believe me, I'm used to doing poor girls' weddings. I know how to make things work on a tight budget. I just thought—" She could not yet hide her wistfulness as her fantasies of a $20,000 wedding started to fade. "I mean with ten bridesmaids..."

"I'm sorry; I don't believe I said that," Molly said. "I'm still in a daze about this and very worried about the expense, but Amanda is insisting on ten and says she's willing to find a way to make it work." In other words, Amanda was stubborn, stubborn, stubborn.

"What do you think you can afford?" Zenith said.

"I don't know," Molly answered, and suddenly she was crying; this was as surprising and just as uncharacteristic of her as her anger had been a moment ago.

"There, there," Zenith said, patting her hand. "I haven't lost a mother yet. Have some more herbal tea."

"Thank you," Molly sniffed. "It's very soothing, whatever it is."

"It's my own blend. It strengthens the blood. I gave some to Bonnie when she was in the hospital from when Luke shot her. I think that's why she recovered so fast, although of course those smarty-assed doctors think they cured her."

"Bonnie. Oh Zenith, you're her aunt, I forgot. Did anybody tell you what's happened?" Betty said.

"To Bonnie?"

"Luke's escaped from jail."

Zenith clutched her face. "That's awful. Is there no end to what that girl has to suffer? When did this happen?"

"John got a call from the Lima warden about two this morning, but I think Luke was out earlier."

"How'd he escape?"

Betty smiled. "One thing they never like to tell, not

even to other police, is how an escape was done. Don't want too many people knowing that skill, now do they? John's got a deputy over guarding Bonnie, but let's be watchful, yes?''

Zenith nodded thoughtfully. Then to Molly she said, ''Amanda's coming in tonight? Do you two want to come over here tonight to talk?''

''Maybe. Can we call you? Last I talked to her, she wanted to meet tomorrow afternoon at our house with some of the bridesmaids. If she does want that, would you join *us* instead?''

''I'll bring my daughter. She usually helps with the weddings.''

AMANDA'S CAR was already in the drive when Molly got home. She raced inside, eager to see her daughter, who hadn't been home since Christmas. Amanda was on the floor playing with puppies. There was always a puppy or two in the West home because Molly and Ken were foster caregivers for the local Puppy Rescue Association, an organization that salvaged abandoned puppies, nursed them to health, and put them up for adoption. Amanda jumped up and hugged her mother. Then the two women settled back down on the kitchen floor.

With a quick glance it would have been hard to tell mother and daughter apart. Amanda was taller than her mother, her figure more willowy. Her face, like her mother's, was attractive when animated, but when still, as when she studied it in a mirror, she thought her jaw was a bit too large and her eyes too widely spaced. Amanda hid these flaws with wildly flowing dark brown hair that she was fond of handling with her long artist's fingers. Amanda's habit of crunching or twisting her tresses was as much to display her hands as her hair.

Molly had long since surrendered her own flaws to the conveniences of a pageboy and bifocals. She had also accepted her thickening waist and arms with fiftyish calm, but was still thin enough that the young woman she had been was evident, especially when she sat beside her daughter.

Amanda had brought a bag of rawhide chips with her, and both puppies were aggressively trying to figure out what to do with them.

"These two are supercute. What? Beagle and basset mix, perhaps?"

"Dad thinks maybe a touch of cocker spaniel."

"Wonder if I can talk Bently into letting me have one."

"They're both really smart; they'd be easy to train."

"I know, I'll tell him I'm getting both, then 'agree' to only take one. That'll win him over. He likes animals. He's just not used to them."

"I can't believe you two are finally going to marry."

"I figured you and Dad lived together three years. Why should we break your record for noncommitance?"

"But why such a rush? Two months isn't much time to put together a wedding."

"Because—"

A pickup crunched into the drive and braked sharply. Mother and daughter craned necks to see over the windowsill.

"Matins," Molly said. "He talked to me earlier. He needs your help."

"Oh no, not a brochure. People have no idea how much time those 'little' design favors take."

Matins stepped to the porch and through the door saw

them on the floor. "Credit company repossess your chairs?" he said. An Appalachian hello—an insult.

"Hello to you, too," said Amanda. "As always, it's a pleasure to see no one's shot you yet."

An Appalachian reply—a bigger insult. Because there was only one school system for the whole Tricounty, Amanda, a professor's daughter, had mixed enough with regional children to pick up the rhythms of their speech, including the accent, the syntax, and the adeptness with insults.

"Do I get down there or do we all go find chairs?" Matins said.

"Mom says you want a favor. I'm here playing with these puppies. You want to ask me to go and do something, you'd better get down with these here pups, too."

"Sassy. She really your child?"

"No. Switched at birth. Not ours," Molly said.

He sat down and grabbed a puppy. "Where's your big dog?"

"Goldie? I don't know," Molly said.

"Don't worry, Dad took her with him. He went to the grocery store I think," Amanda said. "So what's this big favor you need?"

"Me? Don't need nothing. But I want you to help Bonnie Siever."

"Bonnie? She's to be my matron of honor. Did Mom tell you? Is something wrong with Bonnie?"

"Luke Siever's escaped from prison," Molly said. "John thinks she's in danger and wants her to go stay with you."

"Just until he's caught," Matins said. "I can put a deputy to guard her house, but I won't really feel she's safe unless she's out of town somewhere where nobody knows. I figured you're good enough friends with her not to be too inconvenienced. I especially don't want Bonnie's ma to know where she is.

"Why not?" Molly said.

"She'd blab," Amanda replied scornfully.

"When do you go back to Cleveland?" Matins said.

"Sunday night, but I could go back in the morning if you think it necessary."

"Well, let me think this through. Maybe I'm overreacting. Maybe a deputy's enough."

"Not sure *I'd* feel safe with those guys on guard," Amanda said.

"Amanda—" Molly started to rebuke her rudeness.

"No, she's right," Matins said. "My deputies aren't top-of-the-class academy types are they? Well, we'll solve this somehow. I'll call you soon as I've talked to Bonnie. Tell Ken to call me," he added with a knowing glance toward Molly.

"I think let's go see Bonnie now," Amanda said to Molly when he'd left.

"I agree. Leave a note for Dad. He worries."

BONNIE HAD BEEN LIVING with her mother since Luke went to jail. She couldn't afford to keep up the trailer payments on just her commissions as a cosmetics consultant at the store. It had not been a comfortable arrangement for either, but the size of the house at least gave both women room to avoid each other.

It was about a thirty-minute drive to the Barton Mansion from the Wests' home. By the time Amanda and Molly arrived, Bonnie was in the kitchen, "fussing up" a dinner for them, as the locals termed fancy cooking for company. The kitchen was Amanda's favorite room in the mansion. One wall was modern, with cabinetry, stove, and refrigerator. But the rest was still a nineteenth-century kitchen with a huge six-foot arched fireplace over a step hearth. Twelve-foot ceilings were pricked with dozens of old pothooks, some hung with equally old pots. A trestle table dominated the center of the room and complemented the stone floor. Two antique Hoosier cabinets flanked the floor-to-ceiling windows at one end. These windows overlooked a small mown yard. Behind was dense forest where the Wayne National and Shawnee State Forests ran together and blended seamlessly for thousands of virtually unpopulated acres.

Bonnie glowed to see Amanda. The two hugged; then Bonnie hugged Molly. Bonnie hugged anybody, actually. She was an exuberant personality who laughed and cried easily. Her clear laugh was infectious, as were her ready tears. Like Amanda, she could cry at the sappiest television commercial, so soon the two were happily blubbering, making Molly squirm with embarrassment.

Bonnie was about a half foot shorter than Amanda, with the Partonesque figure Zenith had been troubled by earlier in the day. Her black hair was naturally curly, her eyes deep brown, almost black. Her face was heart-shaped and her mouth matched, so she always seemed puckered as if she were about to giggle or kiss. Her makeup, as befit a cosmetics consultant, was heavy, but professional. She wore wild, dangly earrings of riotous colors, but her outfit was just tight jeans and a plain knit top.

"You look great," Amanda said.

"So do you. I can't believe you're getting hitched finally. I can't tell you how proud I am you want me for matron of honor."

"Of course I want you. You've been like a sister to me."

"You'll be a beautiful bride. You're so tall and thin

with that gorgeous long hair. I can't wait to do your makeup.''

"Bonnie!" Florence Wheeler walked in just then, ready to scold her daughter. "How could you start selling, and they just walked in. How rude.''

"Mama, I wasn't selling. Of course I'm going to do Amanda for the wedding, just as a friend. I wasn't planning to charge. You do want me to do your makeup, don't you?'' she said to Amanda.

"Of course, silly, who else? I wouldn't let anyone else do it.''

FIVE

DISHES

AMANDA AND MOLLY talked a lot in the car as they drove home about three hours later, but not once did they discuss the wedding.

"I'm so proud of Bonnie for standing up to her mother like that," Amanda began as the car pulled out of the drive.

"What?" Molly said, still confused by events of the last few minutes.

"When her ma criticized her for selling makeup to me, remember? Bonnie spoke right up and defended herself. Two years ago, a year ago even, she'd have stood there and taken it. Now she speaks up. Good for her. Luke and her dad had that girl convinced she was worthless. Her ma never hit her, but she's just as bad, always putting her down. Now Bonnie's getting tougher. I used to say to her she could never be free until she learned to sass her ma, and she's finally learning."

"Sassing your ma is the ultimate virtue?"

"You bet. You taught me that."

"I?"

"And a good job you did, wouldn't you say?"

"I'll say. Maybe too good."

"Oh now, maybe we fuss a little."

"A little!" Molly started to retort, then stopped; silly to argue about arguing.

"Hope Bonnie's okay tonight," Amanda continued. "I

didn't see the patrol car there, but she said a deputy'd be there all night. Probably sleep the whole time, the fool.''

"I thought Bonnie was coming home with us."

"No, no, she's going to stay with Florence. Florence is afraid to stay alone until Luke's caught."

"But she said—"

"No, Bonnie will stay there. We'll stop by early tomorrow and take her with us to see Zenith."

"I was sure—"

"No, forget it," Amanda snapped.

Molly, shocked, fell silent, but she knew what she'd seen. Bonnie had set dinner out on the trestle table and the four women had eaten, conversing sporadically about utterly small things, not mentioning Luke or the wedding. Once, to break yet another uncomfortable silence, Molly had commented on the antique dishes. To her surprise, Bonnie began telling her the history of each pattern. One was the last plate in a set the first Clement Barton had stolen from a steamboat of settlers who were heading west in the 1840s. Several of the plates were from a set Esmerelda Barton had bought during a tour of France in 1878 or 1879. Another plate, made in about 1916, was one of the more famous Limoges rose patterns. The Wedgwood serving platter once had belonged to a branch of the Patrick Henry family.

"These must be priceless," Molly had said.

"Not quite," Bonnie had replied with a strange smoldering look toward her mother.

"Dammit, Bonnie," Florence had abruptly exploded. "They're just dishes." Then she'd grabbed a saucer and smacked it against a chair. As the porcelain fragments fell against the stone floor, they clanged with an exquisite medley of pure tones, intensifying the shocked silence of the other three women. Then Bonnie started to wail and ran sobbing from the kitchen. Amanda followed her.

Florence, still furious, gathered up the remaining dishes and began washing them with a delicacy usually reserved for a tub of Tupperware. She didn't break any, but Molly, who dried, winced every time Flo slammed one into the dishrack. Neither woman spoke.

Florence was a withered woman, probably about Molly's age, but she looked much older because a two-pack-a-day cigarette habit had shriveled her skin. Her hands, too, were wrinkled and darkened, matching her face. Her hair was black like Bonnie's but streaked with gray. Her clothes were at odds with her troubled body; they were expensive—wool slacks, silk blouse, gold earrings, fine kid leather shoe boots. She was one of those country paradoxes, a poor woman's body and a rich woman's clothes.

Molly finally tired of the tension and attempted to start a conversation. "So what do you do when Bonnie's at work?" she'd said. She was trying discreetly to ask if Flo had a job herself.

"Mostly clean up after that worthless girl."

"Oh, Bonnie has lots of spunk and charm," Molly had replied.

"That's why she's so damned much trouble."

"She fixed a very nice dinner. She's a very good cook, wouldn't you say?"

"Spend all her money on her worthless friends, I'd say."

"That worthless friend of hers, Amanda, happens to be my daughter," Molly had said, as gently as she could, but she was rapidly tiring of Flo. No matter what the woman's troubles, couldn't she find a little civility inside that hardened husk?

As Molly dried and stacked the plates, she continued thinking in silence. Perhaps it took courage not to be bitter after a bitter life. What would I be like without Ken? A terrible thought. He worries too much and is sloppy about the checkbook and is always forgetting things—yet isn't he there when I need him? Doesn't he listen when I talk to him? No, I can forgive Florence, Molly thought. I can afford to.

Florence had been the only child of Clement Barton V and Lois Milvane Barton. Her mother had been active in the Ohio Daughters of the American Revolution and three times president of the Esmerelda Barton Chapter of the Ohio First Families Association. Lois displayed her historical relatives, Milvanes and Bartons, good Bartons that is, the way some people displayed lawn ornaments. To Florence it seemed as if Lois valued dead relatives more than a live daughter. Florence learned how to pour tea and dress properly for dinner, but what she really wanted was out. Like her sister-in-law, Zenith, she had escaped by marrying a Wheeler. It got the results she wanted; David Wheeler appalled her mother.

But unlike Zenith, Florence never seemed to repent of marrying a Wheeler. David was exciting, with his big Harley and dual tattoos on his arms. They'd roar together over the winding back roads, Florence letting her long black hair stream out behind her. She thrilled to press against him when he leaned into those tree-draped curves. He took her dancing to clubs her mother would disapprove of if she even knew they existed. The music was raucous, the smoky lights as sexy as the musicians. Each had a story. David played an occasional bass, so they all knew him; at breaks they'd come to their table, buy her a drink, and talk about their gigs, honky-tonks, and women. They'd all been to Nashville, New Orleans,

Memphis. Exciting places. Drunks? Deadbeats? Losers? No, they were people with lives. They'd been *out* of Ohio. Of course she married David. He gave her the world.

She'd really loved him, even after his beatings caused a miscarriage. During her second pregnancy, with Bonnie, he'd behaved, and she'd thought he'd changed. Having a baby seemed to gentle him; he'd loved rocking the infant, holding her, cooing. Then when Bonnie was about eleven months old, something snapped, and he'd become the violent David Wheeler again. Not all the time, just often enough to make Florence afraid of him. He became suspicious of her every move. They grocery-shopped only on Saturdays so he could go with her and watch her to be sure she didn't flirt in the aisles with other men. He wouldn't let her have a car or work because she might meet men and thus become wanton.

The only way she could get out of the house was to get on the school bus in the morning with Bonnie. When she did that, she'd spend the day walking up and down the streets of New Forge looking at people's flower gardens. Because the town was built on steep hills, the streets switched levels at every block. Basements overlooked nearby rooftops or garages were sometimes on a house's second floor. The terrain, which accounted for some spectacular foundation cracks, also engendered highly creative gardening. Town gardens tiered yellow somethings above red other things; magenta daisylike things with ferny leaves spilled into tiny, intensely blue something-elses. Florence walked among these displays, wishing she knew the names of the somethings, but afraid to ask anyone for fear they'd tell David where she'd been while he was at work.

Those walks ended when one day David came home

from work early and found her gone. She ended up in the emergency room after that beating. A nurse tried to talk her into going to the battered women's shelter, but she wouldn't. Perhaps she believed she deserved the beating. She never got on the bus again. She bore all this because, as she told her daughter, being married was a duty and a privilege. She never seemed to forgive Bonnie for testifying against Luke. It wasn't right for a woman to speak against a husband, in Florence's view.

As a woman whose self-worth had been based so totally on being married, she was utterly devastated when David left her. "For another woman," the note said, "one who can truly love me." Sheriff Matins had taken the note for the missing persons' file, but, as he told Molly and Ken over dinner a few nights after the disappearance, he wasn't going to look too hard. Flo was better off without him.

"Not your right to judge," Ken had rebuked.

"Maybe not, but this will save the county money. I can't tell you how many times we've had to go out there and calm them down."

"Who calls?"

"Bonnie usually."

There were fewer calls after Bonnie married, but Flo began looking worse than usual, too. Molly watched the woman swirl the suds and her annoyance cooled to pity. She had learned most of Flo's life story from Amanda or the sheriff. Matins, perhaps inappropriately sometimes, confided in Molly and Ken. Maybe he did so because Ken, as a criminologist, or more precisely as a sociologist who taught a single course in criminology per year, was about the closest thing Matins had to a peer in the Tricounty. Molly cherished the trust he had in them, whatever his reasons, but it also meant that occasionally she found herself standing beside someone, helping her with the dishes, and knowing too much about her.

"There," she said. "Last one done. Wonder where those girls are?"

On cue, the two burst in laughing, though Bonnie's eyes were still red from her tears. "I'll get some things," Bonnie had said. "Meet you outside."

"Right," Amanda said. "Come on, Mom, I've got to hurry to be home for Bently's nightly call."

Molly had hurried. She couldn't wait to get away from Flo.

"Let's go," Amanda said, getting into the driver's seat and starting the car.

"But," Molly said, "where's Bonnie?"

"Bonnie? What makes you think she's coming?"

"But she said—"

"Hurry, Mom, I've got to get home."

KEN WAS ON THE PHONE when Amanda and Molly entered the kitchen. "Oh Dad, please, Bently's about to call," Amanda said.

"This *is* Bently," Ken said. "We've been having quite a chat. I didn't know Bently was his mother's maiden name."

"Thanks, Dad. Hi, honey…" Amanda said into the phone.

"And do you know what else?" Ken said, but now only to Molly since Amanda was lost in various sweet nothings and would have no interest in her parents for a while. "His family invented the window screen. They had been making flour sifters with horsehair mesh when they got the idea to stretch mesh across a window frame. But they couldn't get enough horsehair to meet the demand, so they thought of using wire mesh instead. They had to invent the extruding machine to make the fine wire for mesh. The product was really popular and had the firm securely positioned in metals just in time for the Civil War. Isn't that interesting?''

"Does the company still make screens?''

"I didn't ask. Rats. No use interrupting that pair for something so unromantic as family history. Come, look what I've been doing while you were gone.''

He'd built a fire in the living room. On the couch, on the coffee table, and even on the floor were dozens of computer printouts.

"You've been surfing again?'' Molly said.

"Yeah, and guess what topic?''

She shrugged.

"The paramilitary movement, especially in Ohio. I don't believe how much I found in a little less than two hours on-line.''

"You must have talked to Matins. It scares me to death to think something like that would be right here, right in our area,'' Molly said.

"Well, two hours' research is a pretty flimsy basis for any kind of theory, but I'm starting to think I'm less scared of their violence than I am of our violence toward them,'' Ken said.

She looked at him. His face was as serene as usual. Nothing in his expression suggested he'd been examining the rantings of evil conspirators. He was barefoot, in comfortable jeans and a knit shirt. On first glance, with his slightly thinning hair and slightly rounded paunch, he looked to be an affluent, middle-aged householder relaxing at home before a cozy fire. On deeper glance, however, she saw instead Dr. K, the professor, puzzling through stray bits of information to make sense of them, sociological sense, as if he were writing a lecture, which he probably was.

"Which course?" she said with a teasing smile.

"What?" Then he grinned. "Oh, am I sounding like 'the professor' already? Well, you're right, I'm thinking about doing something on the militia movement, probably in my Social Problems course. But I tell you, the pattern for U.S. fringe movements is, we as a society have less to fear from the fringe than we do from overreaction by the middle. Our fear, our middle-class fear, so often unnecessarily persecutes cranky but essentially harmless people. That may in the long run do more harm than those cranks might, mainly because it drives people to their cranky causes."

"I'm sure the people who buried loved ones after the Oklahoma City bombing just love to hear people like you dismiss their pain."

"No, no. I'm sorry to have said that so crudely. My thinking is still fuzzy. Two hours' work isn't enough for clear thinking, but I tell you that's what I saw. I saw a real danger from the center, a new McCarthyism. McCarthyism has always been the biggest ism in this culture. Most of the hysteria on the Web is not by the lunatics. It's from the good guys."

He saw Molly's wide eyes and backtracked. "Okay, I'll just tell you what I did; you decide what it means. I sat down after I talked to Matins and played around. I started on the Web. I also spent some time on a text-only version of a network of Ohio university libraries called OhioLink. I didn't find much in the social science databases, so I used newspaper and magazine abstracts instead. I found most of these abstracts and all of the Web pages using the Boolean syntax Ohio and Unorganized and Militia and—"

"Whoa, Ken, I'll make a deal with you, I won't teach you double-entry bookkeeping if you don't teach me computer network skills."

He laughed. "Okay, forget all that. Anyway, I found a ton of pages by and for the militia types, but most of it is social. There are dating services, even. People who stumble across these pages might think, if the Web were their only source, that militarists are just a bunch of people who like to dress up in funny garb, go camping, and play games in the woods."

"Sort of like Civil War reenactors?" Molly said.

"Oh my, I hadn't thought of that. Our Amanda a right-wing commando? My little girl a gun nut?"

"I don't think so," Molly said. "At least I hope not."

"There's a Web page by a group here in southern Ohio that brags how apolitical they are, they're just working on their woodland skills, just a bunch of buddies getting together, and for twelve dollars they'll be very happy to send me their apolitical newsletter."

"There's a militia here in southern Ohio?"

"Oh, several, and all have slick Web pages, slicker than those of most universities. Great graphics, great search engines, great links, whatever else you may think of these groups, you have to admire their mastery of on-line media."

"Did you subscribe to that apolitical newsletter?"

"You kidding? Of course not. But I did visit all the links they posted. To read Web pages of militarist groups, all seems reasonable, just Mom and apple-pie friendly." Ken was in his let's-be-rational mode, obviously.

"Well, of course." Molly, on the other hand, maybe because of the unfinished argument with Amanda, was suddenly in a let's-argue mode. "Of course they're sweet and pious. The *Communist Manifesto* after all, can be read as a document of peace, love, and brotherhood, never mind those cuddly concentration camps. So can the Bible, and look how many people have been killed for Jesus."

"Funny you should mention Jesus. That's what the other side, the antimilitia Web pages say. All those pages purporting to reveal the 'truth' about militias warn about the religious ideology of the movement. They argue that militia groups believe in the ideas of Christian Identity, a church started in Los Angeles in 1948 and which believes there are two races on earth: a godly race descended from Adam and a satanic race fathered by the devil."

"Let me guess. Satan's children are black."

"And Jews."

"Convenient."

"But there's another tenet, again remember this is from some antimovement documents. They claim that the militia types believe the Constitution and Bill of Rights were divinely inspired doctrines, written by God through the Founding Fathers. Therefore, they are holy texts, not to be revised by mere men, so any amendments, beginning with the Thirteenth, are illegitimate. So no women's suffrage, no income tax, no outlawing slavery."

"What about the Eleventh and Twelfth?"

"I haven't figured out why those are okay with God and the rest aren't. But what I'm really trying to tell you, all this information is coming from antimilitia on-line sources. And it's all assertion, not fact. The only fact I've seen is that Wesley Swift started the church that became Christian Identity in 1948 and even that fact is just asserted, not attributed to any source."

"So because none of these documents uses approved academic footnoting style, you're dismissing them?"

"Ouch. Claws out tonight aren't they? No, I'm just saying maybe it's too hasty to be afraid; maybe what we need is to be informed. And the Internet is not the place for reliable information. One thing for sure, these groups are more different than similar. The right wing is hardly monolithic or united with any specific Christian sect. The only generalization I feel safe making at the moment is the movement is talkative, but talk is not violence. An unreasoning fear of talk can destroy a society."

"Well, I'm sorry. I'm afraid," Molly said. "I don't like the idea of guys with guns running around in the woods, the woods behind our house maybe. I'm sorry if that's unreasoning. It seems like common sense to me, though."

"Well, sure, a fear of violence is rational, but the more I read this stuff, the more I think the violence comes from normal sociological stressors and not from the right wing itself."

"I don't follow you."

"People gripe about government all the time. Few act on these complaints with bombings or murder. The few who do suffer from other pressures that can explain their behavior, psychological disorders or family dysfunction being the main two. For better or worse, mostly worse in my opinion, right-wing ideology on the Web may be what lots of people think nowadays. But thinking something and shooting someone are seldom linked. Most violence is family violence. Ideology rarely stimulates violence."

"You're saying the people who bomb come from weird families?"

"I'm saying family violence may explain more of these dramatic incidents than does ideology. Just look at the statistics." He handed her another printout.

"Also from the Web?"

"Yes, but you'll notice it uses correct citation style."

"Ah, citation syntax, the liturgy of scholars."

"Read the numbers."

She read: Twenty-four percent of American women have been hurt or injured by physical abuse at one time in their lives. Thirty-four percent of Americans have witnessed an incident of domestic violence. Child abuse and domestic violence account for one-third of the total $450 billion cost of crime in the U.S. each year. Abused children are more likely to be involved in violent criminal activity in the future than their nonabused peers.... There was more. Molly sat with the sheets in her lap for a minute. Then she shook her head firmly.

"Ken, I'm not convinced. There have been too many paramilitary incidents—Waco, Ruby Ridge, Oklahoma City, the Texas Republic, the Arizona Viper Movement. There's a poison in the country. Something's wrong with these fringe types. They're dangerous."

"But so are our reactions to them," Ken countered. "Here, from the *Houston Chronicle*. After Waco, over 440 militias were formed throughout the nation according to the Southern Poverty Law Center's Militia Watch. It's an action/reaction thing. Every time there's a radical-right atrocity and every time it's met by a massive federal action, the whole cycle escalates. Nut plus frenzy equals more nuts, more frenzy, but my point, the nuts start out as genuine nuts. Here from the *LA Times,* a profile of Richard McLaren, who was the so-called ambassador of the Republic of Texas. He was, according to the story, actually from St. Louis, but he was obsessed with the Alamo; it went back all the way to a third-grade book report. He believed his own mythology. McLaren was so extreme that his republican group impeached him a few days before the shoot-out. It might have been this rejection that led to the violence, not his beliefs. In short, we're looking at psychological causes, not ideological.''

"But no psychotic announces in his manifesto that he hates his mother,'' Molly protested. "He cites dogma, doctrine, ideas that he gets from those selfsame Web pages you've been looking at.''

"True, but do we abolish the dogma, thus condemning millions of innocent people along with, or do we try to understand the minds of those few who destroy? Let's toss away all this junk from the Net. Everything we need to know I teach in Beginning Sociology.''

"Oh no, Ken, don't you dare.''

"There are four levels of violence: One, verbal aggression, such as insults and yelling; two, physical aggression, such as shoving and pushing; three, severe aggression, such as beating or punching; and, four, murder, the ultimate violence.''

"The Appalachian insult is a local art form. Are you saying we live in an aggressive culture?''

He looked at her, surprise on his face. "Molly, what a great theme for a paper. I can see the title now: 'The Backwoods Insult as Significant Social Attractor Factor for the Unorganized Militia Movement.'''

"Ooh, 'attractor' and 'factor' in the same title; good show. But where's the colon? Have to have a colon in academic titles.''

"Right, damn. Well, I'll work on it.''

"I've always seen the insult as just local humor.''

"Me too. I'm going to have to think about this. The insult is a daily norm; you can't succeed in this culture without skill at verbal abuse. You may really have stumbled onto a genuine reason why the militia movement has so much local appeal.''

"So there are four types of violence?" Molly prompted.

"And two models to explain violence, the psychological and the sociological."

"Models? Why wasn't 'model' in your title?"

"You're right; if I use 'model,' I can probably get the colon, too. Wait, wait it's coming: 'The Backwoods Insult Factor—*colon*—A Social Attractor Model for the Appeal of the Appalachian Unorganized Militia.' There."

"Applause. Applause," she said.

"Okay. Now behave, I'm actually trying to tell you something important, something that will help Matins. So hush and listen. Uh, please, of course. It's not verbal aggression, if you say please."

"Of course."

"The psychological model sees violence as a disorder in the individual. The sociological model doesn't reject that; it adds to it some social and economic factors to explain violence. The sociological model argues that the need to control combined with poor social resources causes all violence."

"All violence?" Molly said sweetly.

"Yeah," Ken said, but cautiously. He'd been kayoed by that tone of voice before.

"So if you're frustrated and bossy, you're violent?"

"Ouch. Succinct. Brutally so. But yes. Except the higher levels have additional explanations. The second level, adult slapping and shoving, usually is learned from a violent role model, say, experience as an abused child. And the other two levels, beatings and murder, almost always involve a severe personality disorder or extremely low self-esteem. I can support this with citations if you like."

"No, I just want to know if any of this is going to be on the test."

"You better believe it. Look, I can condense this down to one thought. You and the sheriff will be more likely to find your smuggler if you look for a criminal, not a political group. Look for someone with a history of violence or criminal behavior. If militarists are involved, they're being used by the criminals, not the other way around. But if you bring in a commando force to go after a political group, all you're going to do is increase local paranoia and help the recruiting efforts of these groups. What's more, I doubt that you'd stop the gunrunning. If a lifetime studying social behavior means anything, then your smuggler is a criminal first and a militarist second, if at all."

"So we're looking for someone who's frustrated, bossy, abused as a child, low in self-esteem, and maybe skilled at wisecracks."

"I think so."

"Well, thank you so much. That really narrows it down to, oh, half the human race."

"Your enduring respect for the social sciences is, as always, gratifying."

"I'd have more respect if once, just once, it would produce something useful."

"How about this?"

"How about what?"

"I researched another topic while waiting for my absent true love to finally wander home." He handed her yet another two printouts.

"Crochet?"

"Thought you'd be interested. I was surprised by what I learned. Did you know crochet is a totally American craft, invented by the Pima Indians, who were the first to make fiber chains with their fingers? Irish frontier women adapted the craft by adding hooks, probably broken sticks with nubs on the ends at first. It differs from ordinary lace making because it's worked in the air instead of on a work surface. I really think it's ironic that in this country it's called by an Old French word meaning 'hook,' but in the rest of the world it's called American lace. Anyway, happy Valentine's Day, more or less on time, for once.''

She smiled, genuinely pleased at the gift, but, truth be told, she didn't see how knowing that you could crochet with a broken twig was in any way useful either.

SIX

MAIL

IN THE MORNING the phone rang. Early. Molly answered it. Florence.

"I need to speak to Bonnie; something terrible's happened," Florence said.

"But Bonnie's—"

"—will be right home." Amanda had grabbed an extension. "We were just about to leave."

"No, I need to talk to her."

"She's already in the car," Amanda said. "Florence, whatever it is, it'll wait until we get there."

Amanda slammed down the phone. "Mom, come on, hurry. We've got to go."

"Amanda, what is going on?"

"Mother, don't start."

"Start what? Amanda, either tell me what's going on or leave me out of your shenanigans."

"In the car; I'll explain. We have to hurry."

"Ken, we're going," Molly hollered. He was still asleep. "Ken, we're going; the puppies need out. So does Goldie."

"Okay, Amanda," Molly said as she latched her seat belt. "No more games. Level with me. Where's Bonnie?"

"In a cave."

"Ugh. Where?"

"Under the house; we never told you or anyone. Especially, we never told Bonnie's parents. There are a whole series of caves and tunnels under there, used for the Underground Railroad and Prohibition. We fixed one up when we were in high school. That's where she'd hide to avoid being beaten or to get away from her ma's nagging. I hate that woman. She's as abusive in her way as that father was. Thank God he's gone.''

"So Bonnie hid in the cave all night?''

"Yeah, we figured it was one place no one knew about. She said she'd never shown the caves to Luke or even told him about them. She said as far as she knew, she and I were the only ones who knew about our cave. Even though Florence grew up in the house, I figure she is such a fraidy she's probably never explored them.''

"But why not come home with us?''

"Florence would tell Luke that's where Bonnie was. If Luke did come meaning to kill her, he could find her at our house.''

"I never thought; we were in danger last night, too.''

"I don't think I slept a wink last night. You never knew, never saw what I saw,'' Amanda said. "Luke Siever is as nasty as David Wheeler.''

"Poor Bonnie. She never gets a break, does she?''

"Maybe I should go home today and take her with me. We can plan this wedding later.''

"Wonder what's happened that made Florence call so early.''

"Probably a spider in the bathroom. Flo just likes to manipulate Bonnie; doesn't like not having Bonnie there to push her buttons. Okay, now that you're in the know, Mom, you're in the plot, too, right?''

Molly grinned. "Sure. Believe it or not, I'm the adventurous type."

"You?"

"Oh, I could tell you a story or two. Ask your father about my cockfighting days."

"What?"

"So what do you want me to do in this plot of yours?"

"You go in and keep Florence talking while I fetch Bonnie."

"Typical, you give me the hard part, and you do the fun stuff. I'd like to see these caves."

"I promise, when Luke is recaptured, we'll show them to you. Only you are honor-bound never to tell anyone about them, not even Dad."

"I promise. Women should have secrets. Especially mothers and daughters."

"Yes, but not with each other." Amanda laughed.

"Oh, especially with each other, I think," Molly replied.

Florence sat on a porch railing, still in her gown. She picked at a piece of trim. "So terrible, how could these things happen to me?" she was muttering.

"What is it, Florence?" Molly said.

"Where's Bonnie?"

"She's coming; she's getting her things," Molly said. "Now tell me what's wrong."

"No, I need Bonnie."

"Well, let's get inside and get you dressed at least. I'll make some coffee. Do you want me to help you dress?"

"No."

By the time Florence came back downstairs, the smell of coffee filled the house. Bonnie and Amanda soon followed, Bonnie looking pale and tense. Perhaps she expects Flo to restart last night's argument, Molly thought.

"There, that package came for you," Flo announced when she saw Bonnie.

"So early?"

"I forgot to check the mailbox yesterday afternoon, so that package has been in the box all night."

"Oh. But it's been opened," Bonnie said.

"I didn't know when you'd be home and I couldn't wait; I was just too curious."

"Florence! Aren't you ashamed?" Amanda said. "Opening other people's mail? That's illegal."

Florence hung her head. Bonnie, holding her coffee in one hand, pulled aside the wrappings and then dropped her cup. In the box was a black handgun. "Bonnie, Beware," was crayoned in crude letters on a card underneath.

"Don't touch it," Molly gasped.

Bonnie stared dumbly at her since, well, she was already holding the gun in her hand.

"I mean, put it down and don't touch it again. To protect any fingerprints on it."

"It's a toy," Bonnie said. "It's just plastic."

"But it looks so real," Amanda said.

Florence once again was picking at her clothes. "Bonnie, that coffee will stain the carpet."

"Oh, sorry, Mother. I'll mop it up."

Amanda's face flamed, partly at Bonnie for apologizing, partly at Flo for fussing about her carpet at such a time.

"I'll see if the deputy is still here," Molly said. From the porch she walked down the steep gravel drive. This was one of those rare February Saturdays that was crisp, sunny, and calm. How could there be trouble in the world on such a day? The deputy's car was hidden in the brush at the bottom of the drive, and the deputy himself was in it, snoring.

"Zntz? Oh hello, Molly, long night."

"Yes, I just bet you've been awake every minute, Deputy Connors. Quick, radio John."

"Luke's here?"

"No, just his handiwork."

"Are you going to tell him I was, you know, kinda dozin' like? Because I swear, Molly, I didn't sleep any until a minit ago."

When Molly came back inside the others had erupted into a full-fledged quarrel.

"If you'd not testified, none of this would be happenin'. I told you and told you what's right and what's wrong."

"You're not going to start picking on her, Florence, I won't allow it." Amanda was crying.

"You, it's not your business. You, you're the one who's put these unnatural ideas in her head. She's no woman; she's a whore. That makeup she wears. Dating when she's still married. All that reenactment carrying on just to meet men. It's you—you're a bad influence on her."

Bonnie was crying.

"Amanda, please," Molly interrupted.

"Mother, no, it's time Florence realized she can't treat Bonnie like a child anymore."

Molly felt a surge of fury. It reached down, rushing like a fluid through her. "And it's time you realized you're too old to talk to me like that anymore."

Amanda's eyes went wide. And her mouth went shut.

Molly was shaking. Slowly, very slowly, Amanda smiled, and, with softness, said, "Type B has spoken. So be it."

That sentence was one of those family phrases, private and powerful. Amanda and Ken were Type A's, the family had decided during a family conference about four years ago. At the same conference they had decided that Molly and their youngest, Todd, were both Type B's. It had been called a conference, but actually it was a fight. Todd had decided to quit college and the family was against it. Amanda and Ken were yelling at him, telling him how foolish he was being, how shortsighted. In a rage, Ken had turned to Molly and said, "Molly, tell him, tell him what he's doing."

With a look that the two children had always called the tornado look, Molly said, "I think his mind is made up. He's like me."

Ken, who seconds before had been screaming, now quietly said, "Type B has spoken. So be it."

The other three had looked at him confused. "There have been some interesting studies recently—"

The three laughed. They had all just been yelling, but now they were laughing. "Dad and his 'studies,'" Todd said.

"All right, all right, but listen," Ken said. "These studies identify two basic personality types. Type A is quick to show emotion, quick to anger, full of bombast. Type B is just the opposite, slow to anger, rarely shows feeling. Type A men have more heart attacks, but in women—I think this is so interesting—it's the Type B's who have more heart disease. Your mom and I are both heart-attack candidates because she's definitely Type B and I'm Type A for sure. A Type A's anger is as common as breathing; a Type B's anger is very rare, but when a Type B gets angry, it's a life-changing event—divorces get filed, employees get fired, murders happen. I'm definitely Type A, she's Type B. I think the only reason we're still married is she's learned to ignore me when I'm carrying on, and I've learned to listen when she gets mad.''

In the end Todd did drop out for six months and go hiking—alone—in the Rockies. He'd come back, carried extra hours, and graduated on time. Molly understood the whole episode. Type A's are social, but Type B's need to get away sometimes, get to the mountaintop, meditate. She'd be crazy without the woods behind her house for her walks or without those long drives between clients on days she delivered meals. In the silence of the car or the woods, she could hear the silences of her soul. Yes, she understood her son very well. It was her daughter who baffled her.

''I'm sorry, Mom,'' Amanda apologized. ''I'm just upset.''

Molly nodded. ''John's on his way. He'll sort things out. Let's just drink our coffee.'' She was still feeling an unpleasant pollution, the chemistry of anger, in her system. This was another difference between Type A's and Type B's, one she envied. Amanda was already recovered from the uproar, but Molly would be feeling its physical aftereffects for half an hour yet. ''What nice neutral topic can we talk about until he gets here?'' she said.

''Maybe my wedding?'' Amanda suggested.

MATINS SLOWLY, silently, put on plastic gloves, picked up the box and toy gun, then put them in an evidence sack. Molly smiled at the sack. John was an absolute professional. He'd had sixteen years' experience with the state police, including several years training as a detective before running for sheriff. He was good at his work, respected throughout the southern tier of counties, had even won some awards, but as a sheriff in the poorest region of the state, he had to watch expenses. So the "evidence bag" was a recycled plastic grocery bag, the red store logo not quite disguising the gun shape inside. He had half a dozen women in the county saving these bags for him, Molly included.

Calmly, he questioned the four women.

"When does the mail usually come?"

"About three-thirty."

"Who's your delivery person, Eileen McKenna?"

"Yes."

"Does she normally leave packages in the box instead of bringing them to the door?"

"Small ones, yes."

"And you didn't check?"

"The mailbox is at the end of the drive," Florence said. "You see how steep it is. Some days, I just don't check it, especially in winter."

"Has she opened mail of yours before?" Matins asked Bonnie.

"Sometimes."

"You weren't here last night?"

"Well, yes and no."

"What?" Florence said. "You were at Amanda's."

"No, I was here." Bonnie started to cry.

"Tell me," Matins said gently. "Just take your time."

Bonnie glanced first at her mother, then said, "I was in the caves. Under the house, Mother."

"I know about them," Florence said with a strange grimace. "I grew up in this house."

"I spent the night down there, only, Mr. Matins—it's so awful. I, I..." Bonnie put her face in her hands and sobbed convulsively.

"Easy, easy." He had a hand on her shoulder.

"I found a body down there." She was whispering

now, gasping between sobs. "I spent the night there because I was afraid to come up here. I spent the night down there with a skeleton, a horrible, horrible skeleton."

SEVEN

DOORS

FLORENCE FAINTED, spiraling to the floor in a gesture that
needed a hoopskirt for full effect. The fall was wasted
on her beige linen-blend slacks, paisley-print blouse with
shell buttons, and blue-silk designer scarf.

"Molly, you and Amanda stay here with her," Matins
said. "Bonnie, show me this skeleton."

"Please, no," Amanda said. "Mom and I want to
come, too."

"But Amanda," Molly said. "We should help Florence."

"Mom, she's as unconscious as we are. She's play-
acting."

"Go ahead, go on. Don't bother about me," Florence
gasped, a not very convincing gasp.

"Well, if you insist." Molly grinned. She had wanted
to see the caves, yes?

Amanda and Bonnie led Matins and Molly to the basement and down a set of wooden steps.

"No cobwebs," Matins said.

"Now," Bonnie said. "Last night there were quite a
few when we first came down here."

"I had no idea Florence knew about our caves,"
Amanda said. "All these years I thought they were our
secret."

Matins grinned. "Amanda, the whole world knows
about those caves. Steamboat tours on the Ohio River

point out the mansion and tour guides talk about its caves. They've been used by Shawnee, river pirates, runaway slaves, moonshiners, hippies. It's amazing you didn't run into people while you were using them.''

"How do you know all this?" Molly said.

"I took Betty on a stern-wheeler for our thirtieth wedding anniversary. Learned a few things. I grew up here but had to listen to some kid from out of state with a lousy summer job tell me things I didn't know.''

Off to the right at the base of the stairs was a wooden plank door leading to a stone-walled storeroom. Shelves on three sides held paint cans or old canned goods. Ambiguous shapes wrapped in plastic nestled next to tiers of empty margarine tubs. The girls walked to one of the shelved walls and together pushed on the center shelf. With a squeal of unoiled hinges, a section of the shelves swung away.

"Pull that back," Matins said. "Let me see that again." He and Molly stepped up to the shelves. A slight break in the wood was all that suggested the door behind it. The shelves on the right were offset by a half inch, so the wood would slide over the neighboring shelves when the door was opened. "Clever. If you didn't know the door was here, it would be impossible to see from this side.''

"We kept the hinges better oiled when Bonnie's father was here. We didn't want him to hear us. We spent many a night hid here," Amanda said.

Behind the door were more steps, very narrow. Actually they were just four-inch boards set on bare rock. A soft light splayed over them.

"Where is that light coming from?" Matins said.

"There are openings in the riverside walls, some as

small as a hand, some as large as a window," Amanda said.

"So people can get in and out these openings?"

"Not really. Look," Amanda said. They had come to the first "window." Matins stuck his head out and looked down a sheer cliff into a tangle of briars and vines far below.

"Only a mountain climber or a rappeller could get in here, and he'd have to know this opening was here first," Amanda said.

Bonnie added, "Lots of times I've looked up to here from that highway there by the river, see it? Even with binoculars, I can't find these openings. But they provide fresh air and light."

"We found a broken lantern by this one," Amanda said. "We think it was put on the ledge here to give runaways a beacon to aim for."

"So runaways would come through the house like we did?" Molly said.

"I don't think so; would have been too dangerous for the family to have slaves inside with so many bounty hunters combing the woods looking for them. We have another theory, we'll show you," Amanda said.

"There are several rooms with doors here, without windows," Bonnie said. "One of them is the room Amanda and I fixed up. How old were we then, Amanda?"

"Thirteen, fourteen, I guess."

"When had you last been down here?" Matins said.

"It was before I was married. I was married at eighteen, so—"

"Seven years ago, then," Matins said. Molly had heard that tone of voice before. He was thinking. He had an idea. But the girls kept chattering and hadn't noticed the change. "So you used this room to hide from David Wheeler when he was in a temper?"

"Right."

They had come to a human-sized hole with a wooden door blocking it from behind. "This is our room and where I slept last night, but this isn't where I found the body," Bonnie said.

Amanda lit a kerosene lamp, flooding the small room with a warm glow. Two cots and a frayed braided rug were set at center. A set of metal utility shelves on one side was laden with dusty dishes, canned goods, and some games such as Clue, cribbage, Monopoly. "I found one of your old sketchbooks here, too," Bonnie said to Amanda.

"Really? Let me see."

"It's actually cozy," Molly said. "And clean."

"Well, I cleaned it up a bit last night, to pass the time, but it wasn't bad, even with not being used for so long. This door keeps out most critters. I've never found anything bigger than a spider in here."

"Where is the body?" Matins said.

"In another room like this, about five hundred yards down the tunnel."

"Why did you check down there?" Matins said.

"Again, just to pass the time and rekindle some fond memories. We had some good times here didn't we, Amanda?"

"Bonnie and I relived the whole Civil War and maybe a dash of Prohibition down here. It was more than pretend. Sometimes we were runaway slaves in fear of our lives. Sometimes we were frightened Confederate raiders trying to hide from the Ohio militia and get across the river into Kentucky."

"Kentucky was Union," Molly said.

"Just barely, Mom."

The tunnel they were following descended slightly beneath them. "I'm turned around," Molly said. "Are we walking away from the river now?"

"Yes."

"So if we were aboveground, we'd be walking away from the cliff's edge and the mansion into the woods?"

"Yes."

After a few hundred feet they came to another hole with another door.

"This is it."

They opened the door. Amanda held the lantern high. At center of the room, a jumbled heap of stained bones was clearly visible. Nothing else was in the room.

"So seven years since you've been here?" Matins asked.

"Yes."

"You sure they weren't here before."

"Yes."

"Are they human?" Molly said.

"Not sure," Matins said, squatting down, but touching nothing. "Maybe, maybe not."

Molly crouched down, too, and studied the debris in the flickering light. Only parts of bones pricked up through the dirt floor. A roundish shape at one end suggested a skull, but no telling for sure if it was human because most of it was still buried. The bones that did show seemed logically placed next to others. It was an array of bones that had lain together at the moment of death, not the disorder of bones tossed away after a meal.

"You said the Shawnee used these caves?" Molly said.

"So they say," John said.

"Maybe this is a Shawnee burial or even an Adena

burial," Molly said. The Adena were an ancient tribe of moundbuilders who had lived and disappeared from the region over a thousand years ago. The Shawnee were more recent, having been driven out in the more recent genocidal impulse of the American frontier.

"I doubt they're Adena," Amanda said. "As far as anyone knows they buried only in mounds, not caves. But Shawnee's a real possibility. Maybe a warrior fell down a sinkhole and crawled in here to die long before those doors were built."

"An animal could have done the same," Matins said.

"But why wouldn't we have seen the bones before?" said Amanda. "We were all through these tunnels all the time in those days."

"They could have resurfaced recently because of frost heave or even a slight earthquake. Those aren't uncommon here," Matins said.

"So you think it's an Indian or an animal?" Molly said.

"That's a question for a forensic anthropologist. I think that's who we need to call in right now. I know one, a professor at Ohio State University. I'll call him."

"So you don't think it's a body," Bonnie said.

"Maybe it is. Maybe it's not. Let's not leap to conclusions. Over in Athens County a year or so ago, a family found a bunch of bones when they tore out a rotted porch. Folks thought it was a woman and her daughter who had disappeared some years earlier. Paper had a story every day. They practically had the 'murderer' found and arrested until an anthropologist identified them as cow bones. So until we get one here to look, I'd be grateful if you three didn't mention this find to anyone."

"Florence will blab," Amanda said.

"Then we'll just tell her about these here cow bones, won't we?" The girls laughed.

What was he thinking? Molly wondered. Matins stared at the bones a few more minutes, tugging his lip.

"Are there any other entrances to these caves, besides that door under the house?" he said.

"Two that we know about," Amanda said.

She and Bonnie walked a short distance more into the tunnel, bypassing several side passages until reaching a dead end with a hole in the roof. A sinkhole. "We found parts of a decaying ladder over there." Amanda pointed. "We think this is how runaways got down here. They were guided here by an Underground Railroad conductor and climbed down with that ladder. They hid themselves and the ladder during the day and climbed back out at night to continue the journey north. That's our theory, anyway."

"Don't step under the hole," Matins said. Again, he squatted on the ground.

"What do you see, John?" Molly said.

"Mostly pitmarks from rain that's come through that hole. Six years is a long time, isn't it."

"Six?"

"I mean seven."

The second entrance was a crawl hole out onto a ledge on the bluff facing the river. "We've never used this but once," Amanda said. "It's too dangerous. You could, if you were trying to escape from Bigfoot or Shawnee or bounty hunters, climb down this ledge."

"Yeah, we did that once, but never again. It was just too scary," Bonnie said.

"Good Lord, I had no idea you girls were doing such crazy things," Molly said, her face paling.

"Wouldn't it be really cool if the body turned out to be one of Morgan's Raiders?" Amanda said.

"Morgan's Raiders?"

"You guys have to forgive her; she wasn't born in Ohio."

"Neither were you, you sassy girl. Now be polite and tell your ma what she wants to know," Matins said.

"Thank you, John," Molly said. Was that all she had to do to cure Amanda's sassing? Sass her back?

"Morgan was a Confederate cavalier, famous for his raids through Union-held territory. He'd steal supplies and clothing, burn rail lines, cut telegraph wires. He was notorious for daring attacks and even more spectacular escapes."

"In Ohio?"

"No, mostly in Kentucky."

"He was famous for gallantry, too, wasn't he?" Bonnie said.

"Yes. Like once he captured some Union officers and their wives. He was going to send the wives home and send the officers down to prison camps, but one of the wives pleaded and wept so, that he gave the women their husbands back to keep as their 'prisoners.'"

"What'd you tell me about wiretaps, Amanda?" Bonnie said.

"Yeah, this is neat. One of his riders invented the wiretap. Lightning Ellsworth he was called. He was a genius at reading Morse code and discovered that if he put calipers on the wires and held real still he could feel messages going through the wires and no one would know he was listening. So Morgan always knew when supply trains were going through or when troops were near. That's why he always escaped. Ellsworth could even mimic some federal telegraphers' key-tap styles and send fake messages to confuse Union communications.''

"I don't understand.''

"Telegraphers each had distinctive strokes, as personal as handwriting. But Lightning Ellsworth could mimic several well enough to fool the Union command.''

"Why'd they call him Lightning?'' Matins said.

"Ellsworth once kept listening during a thunderstorm and got hit. Didn't kill him, but shook him up a tad. So that's when they started calling him Lightning. Because of him, Morgan pretty much roved with impunity behind Union lines.''

"Until he came to Ohio,'' Bonnie said.

"Right, in 1863 he brought twenty-four hundred cavalry into Indiana and headed east, right through here, looting and plundering all across the southern hills of Ohio.''

"They came by here?'' Molly said.

"Yes, in fact near here there was a hamlet, gone now. Maybe six cabins. They heard Morgan was coming, so they put fresh, hot pies on their windowsills and hid in hollow sycamores. They hoped by this friendly gesture that the raiders would take the pies and spare their homes.''

"Did they?''

"So it's said. They were pretty crazy raiders. They stole food, horses, and supplies, like you'd expect, but they also stole crazy things, birdcages, ice skates, chafing dishes.''

"Chafing dishes?''

"Yeah, it's like they were joking. An arrogant, can't-catch-me attitude. They almost did it, too. This was the farthest north they'd raided, and they got all the way to the eastern edge of the state to a place called Buffington

Island. It was there the Union army finally caught up with them. There was a skirmish; half of Morgan's men were captured, but Morgan himself and the remainder escaped. He couldn't get back over the Ohio River, though, because Union gunboats were all alerted and out in force looking for him, so he headed north."

"He almost made it into Pennsylvania when he was captured," Bonnie added. "They think he might have been trying to join up with Lee at Gettysburg. He wasn't a regular reader of Union newspapers so he didn't know Lee had lost at Gettysburg."

"Yeah, if he had been reading the papers he might have been surprised by his reputation. They always painted him as bloodthirsty, the size of his force was always said to be around five thousand, sometimes as high as twenty thousand. He was supposed to be ruthless. People hearing any noise, like passing cows, would think it was Morgan and run into the cornfields to escape him. People were terrified."

"Sort of an exaggerated terror, much like people feel toward paramilitary groups today?" Molly said.

"Interesting comparison," Amanda said.

"I'd known that stuff about the pies and all," Matins said, "but I'd never known that about the wiretaps before. How'd you learn all this?"

"She's a Civil War reenactor. She knows everything about the Civil War," Bonnie said proudly. "She's a better expert than any of the rest of us in our club, our Damn Yankees club."

"Not anymore, Bonnie," Amanda said. "You've become the expert in these parts. Everyone says so. You know more'n anybody else."

As THEY REENTERED the basement Matins reminded them to keep the find confidential.

"Nothing to worry about, Flo," Matins said upstairs. "Looks like some old cow or deer bones. Prob'ly left from some Shawnee supper."

Molly walked out to the car with him. "What did you mean by that remark, 'seven years is a long time'?"

"It's long enough to erase any marks of a ladder being put down that hole. And it's longer than six years."

"Six, not seven? You think those bones have been there six years, don't you?"

No answer.

"You think they're David Wheeler, don't you?"

"Molly, you're too damn smart for your own good. Maybe they're animal or some raider's bones or maybe they're David Wheeler. My job is to consider all possibilities. So I'm considering."

"But why are you so worried about people knowing?"

"Well, that body, or whatever, might have been deliberately buried and in resurfacing maybe the bones have shifted, too, but the position of the bones makes me think that body was kneeling when it died."

"A murder then?"

"Or an execution."

"Wouldn't there be clothing or something to identify it as human?"

"Not in that clay. It's acidic. Almost any fiber will dissolve in that soil in six years."

"Six, still? Not seven?"

"Molly, you know I trust you. If it's a murder, whoever did it is still here and dangerous. Make sure those two girls keep quiet."

"Well, six or seven, it sure is something old, isn't it?" Molly said.

"I hope not too old to solve," Matins said.

PART TWO

SOMETHING NEW

EIGHT

SNACKS

"WE STILL HAVE the problem of Luke," Molly said. The two were leaning against the cruiser enjoying the unusually warm sun. The bright light made the pines behind the house sparkle.

"I know," Matins said. "Is Amanda planning to go back to Cleveland today?"

"She's torn. She wants to go back for Bonnie, but she'll have to call all her bridesmaids and tell them not to come over this afternoon."

"Rescheduling that group would be a big hassle, wouldn't it?"

"It wasn't easy for her to find a time all those girls could get together, but Bonnie's safety is important, too."

"My Sherry's coming, too?" Sherry was John and Betty's daughter, their middle child, three years older than Amanda and a police officer in Columbus.

"I think she is," Molly said.

"So with me, a deputy, and Sherry here, we'll have plenty of cop power on hand. Maybe I'll have a few state police hang by for a while. Go ahead with the party, only not at your house. You have woods on all four sides. Too dangerous. Too many places for Luke to hide."

"Where then?"

"Here, I think. That cliff in front of the mansion means Luke can only get to the house from the driveway or the woods behind it. Much less for us to watch. Also, since he's put this thing in the mailbox, he's nearby already. So maybe we'll smoke him out by keeping Bonnie at home.''

"Wait a minute, I don't want my Amanda being bait for this setup.''

"Sherry's the best. Everyone'll be safe.''

"No.''

"Let's ask the girls what they think of the plan.''

"Okay, but what makes you think Luke put that toy in the mailbox?''

"There was no postal cancellation on the box and the stamps were wrong for the weight. It was never mailed.''

"I didn't notice.''

Matins grinned. "That's why they pay me the not-so-big bucks. To notice things like that.''

Florence, of course, was against the idea, but Amanda and Bonnie finally wore her and Molly down. If the girls started cleaning immediately and if Molly went to buy the snacks, they'd easily have the house ready in time for a 2:00 p.m. party. Amanda would call everybody right now and tell them about the change in location. Matins would keep a deputy there all day or be there himself. And as soon as Sherry got home he'd send her over. Everything would be fine. Just fine.

Once again, Molly walked Matins to the car.

"How is Sherry doing?'' she asked him.

"Great. She's been promoted again. Going to make detective someday for sure. She's doing undercover work right now, which she won't talk about much. It's probably dangerous, and I'd probably go nuts if I knew what all she did, but I sure am proud of that kid. A cop, like her old dad. Who would have thought it'd be her and not my boys who'd do that?''

"Betty worries."

"Not easy being married to one cop and mother of another. Betty's coming to this confab, too?"

"Yes."

"Well, there's one Saturday where she'll be worrying about something else besides me and Sherry."

He left, and Molly went back in the house, sat down at the trestle table, and started a list. Her first in days. Guess that temper tantrum a while ago really helped. She smiled to herself as she began jotting down items. The girls were already bustling, Amanda on the phone and Bonnie wielding cloths and furniture polish. Florence seemed to catch fire, too, and was happily humming a tune as she cleaned out the refrigerator.

"Mom, be sure to get one of those cheese balls," Amanda said as she hung up the phone.

"Thought of that already, anything else?"

Amanda took the list, nodded her approval. "Guess I'll start vacuuming. Only, wait. Mom, have you ever seen the whole house?"

"No, just the kitchen."

"Flo, may I show her? This is the coolest place. It's like a museum."

Flo nodded. From the kitchen Amanda took Molly down a dark hall, the "servants' hall," she called it. A dining room had mismatched antique dishes placed in no particular array on an oak pedestal table. More mismatched china filled a built-in corner cupboard to overflowing. "I wanted to show you a chest-on-chest in here, but I don't see it now," Amanda said. "Bonnie? Do you know where that chest that used to be here is?" Amanda hollered. Bonnie stuck her head around the door, scowled, shook her head and vanished. Now what's she mad about? Molly thought. Bonnie's mood swings were starting to worry her.

"Florence might have put it in a storeroom," Amanda said. "She was always rearranging furniture when we were little and getting us to help. She loved to do that. Gave her something to do, I guess. It is the neatest chest, stencils on the bottom but on top, original hand paintings by a primitive. Extraordinary. Must be worth a fortune."

Everything looked like it was once very expensive, even when it was new, although now most things seemed seedy and faded. "Bonnie has tried and tried to talk Florence into getting this place listed as a historic landmark and maybe get some of the local historical associations to help restore it. That wallpaper is almost white now, but you can see under the photographs that it was once gold-flocked. And those curtains, they're in shreds now, were once dotted swiss. Bonnie says she found an accounts book in a desk in one of the parlors that said the swiss was bought in 1912, imported from France. I couldn't tell you where to try to buy it now."

"One of the parlors? There's more than one?"

"There's three. They're small, but I think we can get everyone who's coming into the front parlor, by the front entrance."

They walked through these rooms, again filled with Victorian or turn-of-the-century furniture. "Now where's that fainting couch? It was here in the second parlor. I'd never seen one like it. Elaborate hand carving and red-velvet paisley. Incredible. She's moved it somewhere."

Knickknacks, mostly photos and ceramics, covered every flat surface. "One of the aunts, Bonnie once told me, did ceramics, so most of this stuff you see was made, not purchased. We even found the aunt's paint box in a back cupboard."

"I can't believe the chandeliers," Molly said.

"They've never been wired, so if they were cleaned and repaired, we'd have genuine 1850s oil lamps. When these were hung they used whale oil. But they'd burn kerosene, I'm sure. We'll make do for the party with these plain old electric lamps here on the tables. It breaks my heart to see something this wonderful fall into such decay, but Flo just isn't interested in preservation."

Molly picked up a photo. "Do you know who any of these people are?"

"Some. That one is the legendary Esmerelda, the woman who nursed so many runaways and helped them on their way."

"Who's the black woman standing behind her?"

"I wish I knew. To care enough for a black woman to have her sit with them for a photo, what's her story, what's her part in this family's history? A maid? A nanny? I don't know, and Bonnie doesn't either."

"Have you asked Flo?"

"She just always says it's nobody's damn business whenever you ask her about history."

"She's the first, the only Appalachian I've met, then, who doesn't like to talk about family history."

"I know; I can't figure her at all," Amanda said. "Oh, Mom, I've got to show you the upstairs."

"Is that okay? Upstairs isn't for guests."

"Oh, come on."

Molly didn't protest very hard; she was just too curious.

The bedrooms had average, even cheap furniture, perhaps because, unlike the parlors, these rooms were actually used. But Amanda didn't linger over them. Instead she kept going to the third floor. Two large rooms, one on each side of the hall, were filled almost to the ceiling with unbelievable amounts of stuff, just stuff. Molly and Amanda threaded their way among it all, Amanda giddily showing her object after object. Molly was entranced.

"These are hoops for crinolines, this is an old potato masher, these are shoe lasts—in early times they made their own shoes. Notice they're unsided, neither right nor left. This is a hatbox and in it"—she slowly opened the box—"a top hat, probably of beaver. This cradle is hand-made and rough-hewn. Some of this stuff might have been in the family since before the Mansion was built, so that cradle may be from the time the Bartons were living in cabins. Now there's a trunk somewhere in here, I can't find it now. Has she moved that, too? It's full of exquisite quilt tops, never been finished into quilts. But every one a work of art. Oh, wait, here's my favorite trunk." She opened it. "Look."

"Magazines?"

"Not just any magazine. These are *Godey's Lady's Books*."

"I don't know what that is."

"The first American magazine just for women and maybe the finest. Godey wanted a magazine to elevate and improve women's minds, so he published sophisticated articles and fiction in a high-quality format. But most intriguing are these." She opened one carefully to avoid ripping its fragile pages. At its center was a foldout, which when opened showed five colorful gowns. "Intact plates. You see, color printing hadn't been invented then, so these plates, every one, were tinted by hand and then bound in. The workers were all women, they had to sit at long tables all day; each specialized in a color. She would fill in her part and pass the plate on to the next woman."

"Amazing, but how do you know all this?"

"I'm a graphic designer, remember? I studied the history of printing in one of my classes. I did a paper on *Godey's*. Made a special trip down here so I could study originals."

In clambering among the stuff they'd come to a window facing the river. Molly could see Zachariah Point below, then the sparkling Ohio, and beyond, the soft hills of Kentucky. Ohio was thought to be a corruption of a woodland tribe's word, *O-he-yo,* meaning beautiful waters. The hills that lined the river's edges were as beautiful as the water itself and, paradoxically, were identical on both sides, in their arrhythmic undulation and in the monochromatic purity of their February brown. Yet to an African-American in the 1800s, Molly thought, how different those identical riverbanks were. That narrow band of water was one side slave, one side free.

"Well, shouldn't we be getting back to work for this party?" she said.

"Just one more thing, Mom, come."

At the end of the hall was a mirror six feet tall and six feet wide. "This is the only place in the house where the wall was wide enough for this, so the women had to trek up here to check their hoopskirts."

"I never imagined. Of course. In the hoopskirt era, wide mirrors would be needed, wouldn't they?" Molly stood looking at herself and her daughter side by side. Those Victorian women, always stiffly frozen in old photographs, were suddenly very alive as she imagined them primping before this mirror. "For the first time I'm beginning to understand your interest in reenacting," she said.

"I'll have you in hoopskirts, yet, Mom." Amanda laughed.

Just then they heard a scream from downstairs. The

two women tore down the two flights of stairs. Bonnie was standing by the kitchen porch door, which stood open. She held a piece of corrugated cardboard. On it was a hand-drawn heart with a dagger in it and the words, "Bonnie, you better be careful."

Bonnie was ashen-faced, but it was Flo who was screaming.

"Okay, sit down, Flo," Molly said. "Bonnie, where did you find that?"

"In that big urn on the porch. I'd stepped out to shake the dust rag and saw it among the stubble."

"Was it there this morning?" Amanda said.

"Don't know. Could have been. I certainly didn't look there, with all the excitement over the toy gun and the bod—them cow bones."

"Maybe I'd better ask the deputy to stay in the house with us," Molly said.

Deputy Briggs was the officer on duty now, and he readily agreed to come up to the house. If Luke could get up to the porch and slip away again without being seen, then a car in the driveway was too far away for safety. After radioing in his explanations, he followed Molly up to the house. Briggs was an overweight but muscular man and looked tough enough to handle almost anything. He stood at the oversize kitchen windows, his hand on his gun, his face grim, his eyes scanning the woods. Molly smiled to see him playing his role with such exaggerated style. He was the man of the hour, the protector. No felon was going to get by him, no, ma'am, don't you worry none, ma'am. He looked silly, but Molly had to admit she felt safer with him there.

Amanda said nothing, but hugged Bonnie, then went into the front parlor to vacuum. Flo resumed her scrubbing. Bonnie sat at the table, saying nothing. If she had doubts about Matins's plan she was keeping them to herself. But Molly now was full of doubts. Just how dangerous was Luke?

NINE

GIRL TALK

TRUE TO HIS WORD, Matins sent Sherry over as soon as she got home. She banged on the back door of the Barton Mansion about noon. Amanda and Bonnie greeted her with hugs and tears again, but Sherry was more restrained, just a smile and a hello. She had inherited John's taciturn personality as well as his lean frame, although she had Betty's blond hair.

"You look great... I love your hair like that... Have you lost weight?" Such phrases bubbled in the hallway. Girl talk. Molly looked at the trio and shook her head. Girl talk bored her to death and here she was facing hours of it yet. Feeling very sorry for herself, she went back into the kitchen and resumed work on her hors d'oeuvres.

Sherry followed her in. "Mom said to tell you she's bringing Zenith and Dad's bringing Dr. K," she said to Molly. Soon she and Briggs were deep in shoptalk. "We're going to secure the perimeter," she announced to no one in particular, and the two disappeared outside.

About two, the other bridesmaids began to arrive. Dawn Cannon was first, and, unlike the others, she came to the rarely used front door. Amanda hugged her. Bonnie didn't. Odd. Molly thought. Is it because—? Molly was too politically correct even to think the thought, but what she was not thinking was did Bonnie not hug Dawn because Dawn was black? Amanda was laughing as she introduced Dawn to Molly. "I first met Dawn when she walked into a meeting of our Damn Yankees Club and sat down. You can imagine the reaction. Dead silence. A black woman? Here?''

Dawn laughed, too. ''I wouldn't call it dead silence. More like whisper, whisper, whisper. Who is she? Does anyone know her? Where did she come from?''

Amanda took back the story. ''We'd had women from West Virginia and Kentucky before, but never a black woman. I finally asked her why she wanted to come and she just said that there were black infantry units in the Union army. I was real new to my Civil War expertise then and hadn't known that. But she'd had a great-great-uncle who fought at Antietam and one who died at Stone Harbor.''

''This is Bonnie,'' Dawn said softly, picking up the photo of Esmerelda Barton which Molly had noticed earlier. ''I didn't know you had a photo of my great-great-great-grandmother with Esmerelda,'' Dawn said to Bonnie.

''Is that who that is? What's her story?'' Molly said. ''We were wondering about the woman in the photo just this morning.''

Dawn smiled. For someone with a reputation for quietness, she did enjoy being at the center of things. She told the story with relish. ''My great-great-great-grandfather was Zachariah Williams. Bonnie was his wife.''

''The Zachariah Williams?'' Molly said, truly impressed. Williams Hall on campus was named for him. So was Zachariah Point. Born a slave, freed by will at his master's death, he'd come to southern Ohio and started a shoe factory. He became a daring Underground Railroad conductor who'd slip across the Ohio River on dark nights to help slaves escape from Kentucky. Once he'd stolen an infant right out of an overseer's bedroom. The slave master was keeping the infant hostage in his room at night to prevent his slaves from running away. The mother wouldn't leave without her baby and the father wouldn't leave without his wife, so Zachariah crawled into the bedroom, a knife in his teeth in case the overseer awoke, and spirited the infant away.

Another time, he'd returned to where he'd hidden his boat, only to discover that white bounty hunters had sunk the boat and were waiting in ambush for him. He had, as a precaution, hidden the eight slaves he was escorting in the brush before stealthily approaching the boat, so he saw the ambushers before they saw him. He drew out two pistols from his belt, crawled to the nearest bushwhacker, put a pistol to the man's head and grinned. In the moonless brush, all the man could see were Zachariah's disembodied teeth. He fainted dead away and Zachariah tied him up; the second man was made of sturdier stuff so had to be tied and gagged while he was still conscious, but not before Zachariah ferreted from him where they'd hidden their own boat.

"But my favorite story," Dawn was saying, "is the story of his first abduction. He rescued his sweetheart in broad daylight. She got a pass from her mistress to visit her sister on a neighboring plantation, but instead of going to her sister's she went to Zachariah's old master instead. The son and heir was sympathetic; he and Zachariah had been boyhood friends, so he drove both Bonnie and Zachariah to the Maryland border in a wagon, bold as you please, posing as a young lord taking his slaves on a business trip. The two then walked through Pennsylvania to get here, where he started his shoe factory. Not quite as heroic as some of his later exploits."

"But a lot more romantic," Amanda said.

"Why here?" Molly said.

"This was the iron boom, lots of mines and foundries here. Ironworkers needed special shoes. He was a cobbler by trade. He later made shoes for Union troops, too."

"But what was Bonnie and Esmerelda's relationship?" Molly asked. "To look at the photo you get the feeling they were close."

"They were. Esmerelda named a daughter for her."

"I'm named for that woman, too, because I'm named for my great-grandmother," Bonnie said.

"Bonnie's role is less well-known than Zachariah's. Many people don't know she was Esmerelda's house-keeper, and she tended the runaways in the caves. The slaves hid during the day. Since Bonnie could come and go from the house without suspicion during the day, she could get into the tunnels from the basement to feed them and—"

"Does everyone in the whole world know about our secret caves?" Amanda said, exasperated.

"Secret? Well now, I always wondered why you never mentioned them. You thought they were secret?" Dawn said.

"So it was Bonnie who took care of the runaways, not Esmerelda?" Molly said.

"At first. She could cook for them in Esmerelda's kitchen without other servants being suspicious. Esmerelda didn't even know about it until there were just too many for Bonnie to take care of."

"Bonnie had been stealing Esmerelda's food?"

"No, she always claimed she brought her own. But when Esmerelda found out, she started providing the food, so Bonnie no longer had to buy food for the runaways. Esmerelda was afraid at first, but Bonnie slowly persuaded her to come down into the tunnels and help."

"That's not how the historical association presents Esmerelda," said Amanda. "She was supposed to be this saint, this tower of strength, this supercourageous woman sending runaways on to Canada."

"I'd say Bonnie was the strength and Esmerelda was the support," Dawn said firmly.

"So you've known about those tunnels under the house all this time?" Amanda was practically spluttering.

"My church makes a pilgrimage every February as part of our Black History Month observances. We visit an entrance to those caves in the woods, about a thousand yards behind the house here."

"Your whole church?"

"The whole church."

"Good grief. It is impossible to have secrets in southern Ohio," Amanda fumed.

Dawn laughed, a deep hearty laugh. "Oh, cheer up," she said. "Blacks don't tell whites about those caves. They're secret to most whites, I bet." Amanda started to add something, but they were interrupted by more arrivals, at the kitchen door this time. Florence was just letting the women in as Molly and the other three women reentered the kitchen.

Amanda made the introductions. Mary-Mary O'Dell, another member of her Damn Yankees Club, their fiddler in fact. Her great-great-great-grandmother was a Confederate spy, Amanda explained.

"How do you do, Mary," Molly said.

"Mary-Mary," Amanda corrected.

Mary-Mary laughed. "I have two grandmothers, both living, both named Mary and they hate each other, so my parents hoped using the name twice would persuade each woman that I was indeed named for each."

"You must get tired of explaining that to folks."

"Oh, I do, I do," Mary-Mary said.

"A fiddler?"

"What's a gathering of hill folk without a fiddle? I fiddle at all the camp balls," Mary-Mary said.

"This is Connie Marie Tanton. Do you remember her, Mom?"

"Yes, of course," Molly said. "We went on lots of hikes together when you girls were in high school."

"I'll never forget those, Mrs. West. Is Jennifer coming, too, Amanda?"

"She didn't think so, but she'd like to reunite our art trio." The three girls—Amanda, Connie, and Jennifer St. Johns—used to go on painting hikes together, packing acrylics and brushes, or charcoals and sketchpads. They'd hike in the woods until they found something to paint or sketch. Molly would go with them, carrying sandwiches in her pack instead of art supplies. Sometimes the girls chatted as they drew, but most of the time they worked in silence, concentrating on capturing light and form. Molly would spend the time searching for wildflowers. Seeing Connie again made her think for a minute how much she missed having children at home.

"What are you doing now, Connie?" Molly asked.

"I run a shyness clinic."

"A what?"

"Yes. I've just separated from my husband, so I need a source of income, but couldn't find a job. I took a few courses at Sycamore State, never finished, but in one psychology course I had to run an experiment, and I did one on shyness. The volunteers in my experiment said I'd helped them so much that I've set up a little business in my home to teach shy people to be more assertive."

"Is it a living?"

"No, but it helps supplement the income from grocery clerking."

The two-income rule for Appalachian survival. Molly wanted to ask more about it, but just then Amanda was introducing her to another woman, Ellen McKnight, co-owner of a fabric store and another reenactor. "She designs and even helps make many of our costumes. She's an expert on Victorian dress," Amanda said.

"And here is Lorraine DeWitt," Amanda said, turning to another woman. "Have you met before? We went to high school together, but I didn't get to know Lorraine well until she and I both were accepted to the Cleveland Institute of Art. Lorraine is now an interior decorator in Chillicothe. She's an expert on Victorian homes; I'm trying to get her to join our reenactors group, too, because I'd like us to be accurate in settings as well as in dress. But, silly girl, she thinks she doesn't have time."

"An interior decorator? How interesting," Molly said. "You must have lots of fun."

"Oh, I hate it," Lorraine said.

Molly raised a quizzical eyebrow.

"The phone. I hate the phone. Every time it rings it's some woman who's changed her mind on the wallpaper, who's decided she doesn't like the ottoman, who can't keep her appointment, who thinks I charge too much. How I hate the phone."

"Sounds more like you hate customers."

"It's true, I love the decorating, but I hate other people's tastes, I've got to quit, change. I was asking Amanda about graphic design, and she said if I hate customers, I'd really hate design clients. Every one of them thinks they can do it better. No one respects a deadline. And no one, no one, has taste, she says."

"Amanda said that?"

"Amanda said that."

"Are you really an expert on Victorian interiors?"

"Let's just say I'm very interested."

"Then come look at some of the things here in these parlors," Molly said. "I'm sure Flo won't mind." Molly took her through, much as Amanda had earlier. Lorraine commented with astonishment now and then at some object or other.

"Odd," Lorraine said when they came to the second parlor. "That chair, how it's placed, it doesn't group with any others for conversation. It doesn't look at anything, not a fireplace or a window. Wonder why she's set it like that."

"That does look awkward," Molly agreed.

"See what I mean about no one having any taste?" Lorraine whispered, and Molly laughed.

The party was now in full swing. Bonnie had managed to herd everyone into the front parlor. Flo was carrying trays of food from person to person. Flo actually looked like she was having fun. She'd changed into an electric blue afternoon dress with silver buttons, matching blue shoes, and silver earrings. An Yves St. Laurent scarf adorned her neck. Molly knew it was an Yves St. Laurent; it said so on the prominently displayed label.

Molly took a chair by the front door and swept her eyes around, trying to match each face to its name. Dawn was easiest, but which was Ellen and which Mary-Mary? She heard Bonnie address the shorter woman as Mary-Mary so the other must be Ellen. That one on the sofa, that was Connie, next to her Lorraine. Betty and Zenith had come in; the teenager with Zenith must be her daughter, Pauline. Sherry stood by the doorway to the kitchen hallway. So counting herself, Flo, Amanda, and Bonnie, there were eleven women in the room. Then in the hall she heard Ken's, John's, and Briggs's voices. The three men soon joined them, Ken bellowing, "Okay, where's the food?"

The parlor buzzed with the warm sound of people. Molly glanced at the deteriorating wallpaper. Strange how filling a room with people could so easily restore its energy. For a moment it was 1859, the nation was still innocent, unaware that families could divide, brothers could fight brothers, neighbor betray neighbor and Americans could slaughter Americans in the coming Civil War. As Molly was reflecting, she noticed John, Ken, and Briggs leave for the kitchen.

Sherry grinned and flicked her head toward their retreating backs. "There go your dad and my dad," she said.

"Ah yes, the chromosomal imperative," Amanda said. "No man can stand to stay in a room of women talking. It's a trait written on the Y chromosome. Girl talk! Flee!" All the women laughed.

"Well, now that the guys are gone we can really talk," Amanda said, and the women laughed again. "We're all here except for Amy Faron. She couldn't get a sitter. She won't get here until about four, but let's start anyway." The women sat expectantly, looking at Amanda, who had billed this gathering as a meeting, not a party. What did she have in mind? Molly wondered.

"Mom, for you, Zenith, Sherry, Betty, Connie, Lorraine"—she looked around the room to be sure she had her cohorts straight—"this idea will come as a bit of a surprise. But Bonnie, Dawn, Ellen, Mary-Mary, and Amy when she gets here, you've probably already guessed what I want to do for this wedding. You were some of the earliest members in the Damn Yankees Club. You were there through our first very inaccurate, very poorly planned reenactments, but you were also there when they got better and when we started cosponsoring events with the Ohio 92nd. Do all of you know I met Bently at a reenactment?''

''I thought you met in a photography class,'' Lorraine said. She had been in that same class at the time, she had just been telling Connie a few minutes ago.

''I did, but we were just acquaintances then. We didn't catch fire until we met again at a reenactment the following summer. Neither of us had known we had that in common.''

''Something about a man in uniform, eh?'' Dawn said.

''Well, by then, I was wearing Union blue, too. Got tired of sitting on the sidelines,'' Amanda said.

''I thought reenactors were sticklers for accuracy,'' Lorraine said.

Mary-Mary and Ellen both laughed. ''You want to start a fight among reenactors, just say 'women in the line.' Whoo, do tempers fly over that,'' Ellen said.

''The men forget that women did wear uniforms as disguises to slip through the lines,'' Mary-Mary said. ''My great-great-great-grandmother did that.''

''But they didn't fight, did they?'' Betty asked.

''Probably not,'' Amanda said, ''but I'm not pretending to be a woman in uniform when I dress for battle. I'm pretending to be a soldier; I'm trying to experience what it was like. Why shouldn't it be okay to try to learn, even if you're a woman?''

''So Bently was at this reenactment and you were in uniform. What did you do, shoot him?'' Dawn said.

Amanda laughed. ''No, he was Union, too, at least then. His family, the stories he tells. His family made its wealth in the Civil War. I think he feels personally guilty for that. Anyway, what we want to do is host a public reenactment, with the wedding as the closing event.''

The women shrieked with joy, but Molly's heart sank. How much work would this be? She couldn't imagine getting ready for a public event in two months.

"Where will we do it?" Ellen asked.

"Here, in the woods behind the mansion. There's a public trail access about a half mile down the highway, which could park maybe two hundred cars. We'll set up all campgrounds there, Confederacy, Union, and civilian, including the field hospital, the brothel tent, and the sutlers.''

"Brothel?" Flo said.

"Just pretend, Mom," Bonnie replied.

"Can we get a blacksmith and a carpenter's shop? People like those old-timey demonstrations a lot," Mary-Mary said.

"Dawn knows people who can do period smithy and carpentry," Amanda said.

"Plus we can set up a cobbler's tent with period tools from my family's collection," Dawn said. "But can we do all this on such short notice?"

Thank you, Dawn, for being sensible, Molly thought.

"I've already talked to Kevin—"

"He's the quartermaster for the Ohio 92nd, right?" Mary-Mary said.

"Yes, he said he can arrange the battle, both sides, Confederate and Union, and he even knows a few cavalry that might come, though they might not galvanize."

"They're Confederate?" Dawn said.

"Yes."

"Galvanize?" Molly said.

"Be willing to change sides."

"I still don't understand."

"You never know how many of either side will show up at a reenactment so some soldiers bring both blue and gray uniforms so they can fill in where needed. When they're asked to change colors they're said to be 'galvanized.'"

"Yeah," Bonnie added, "but some people feel strongly about which side they're on. They will only shoot for one side, not the other."

Ellen added, "Especially Confederates."

"It's as if some of them are still trying to win," Amanda said. "They take it too seriously."

"What about West Virginia?" Dawn said.

"I talked to Andy last week of the West Virginia 24th. He said he'd talk to the guys, and he'd also talk to some musicians. They had a band at their last event, with authentic Civil War instruments."

"What about me?" Mary-Mary said. She looked hurt.

"Oh, Mary-Mary, you'll play, too. You are the official fiddler for the Damn Yankees Club. You'll play, I promise. I talked to Kevin again this morning, and he says he has two sutlers interested in coming."

"Sutlers?" Betty said.

"Yeah, suppliers, merchants. In the Civil War sutlers were private citizens who were authorized to set up tents in military camps and sell goods to the soldiers."

"Long as they didn't sell liquor," Dawn said under her breath. Molly was really starting to like Dawn's style of humor.

"Today these are just businesses that specialize in setting up tents at reenactments. Sell about anything as long as it's authentic," Amanda finished.

"Well, or what can pass for authentic. Last time I bought some earrings painted with Victorian floral designs, but they were plastic," Dawn said.

"What did real sutlers sell?" Molly asked.

"Food mostly, the kind of stuff the army didn't supply, like butter, tobacco, maple syrup, stuff like that."

"At exorbitant prices, too," Bonnie said.

"Do you know what was the biggest-selling item?" Amanda said. "Molasses cookies. Isn't that neat? You forget how young these soldiers were. They probably wanted Mom's cookies more than they ever wanted liquor."

"Why do we need sutlers for this event?" Molly asked.

"Food, mainly. They can set up a field restaurant and bar and save us having to worry about feeding people. Course if we have a restaurant, we have to have lavatory facilities, too—"

"No, not in my house," Flo said. "Not hundreds of people traipsing in."

"Relax, Flo, I've already called the state historical association and they'll provide porta-toilets, if we haul them ourselves."

"The sutlers cook the meals?" Molly said.

"Of course."

"And serve drinks?"

"Just beer."

"So guests pay for their own food?"

"Of course," Amananda said.

"So in exchange for making your wedding an accurate nineteenth-century one, we get the wedding itself mostly free?" Molly had begun to smile.

"In effect."

"Do you charge people to come to the reenactment?" As an accountant who hated weddings, Molly thought charging people to come to a wedding had a certain appeal.

"No, no, no. The event itself will be free, but food and souvenirs will be sold by the sutlers. But you're right, staging it as a reenactment will save lots of expenses. The main cost will be costumes for those who don't already have them. But it's not a requirement even to wear a costume. Spectators don't."

"Only, a rule of reenactments is if you aren't wearing a costume, you don't dance at the ball," Bonnie said.

"The way I see it," Amanda said, "is anyone who shows up in a costume is automatically a member of the wedding party. No fussy matching bridesmaids' dresses, just hoopskirts, any color, or uniforms, either side, and you're in the wedding. But we may need something private, too, maybe a light buffet here at the mansion, if Flo allows it. That is where you come in, Zenith, you do the buffet. Everything else, I thought, would be part of the reenactment, even the flowers, we'll just pick forsythia or something."

"I'm not sure…" Flo began.

"Please, Mom," Bonnie said. "Think of it, a real Civil War mansion for a real Civil War wedding."

"Please, Flo. The buffet would only be for immediate family and friends," said Amanda. "We've had that many or more here when we've had those teas you used to let us do."

"What about the invitations?" Molly said.

"I thought a few handwritten personal notes to people who won't be interested in the reenactment, Bently's parents and stepparents, for example. But for everyone else we'll just rely on normal publicity techniques, press releases and a home page on the Web. And we'll let whoever comes be whoever comes."

"The wedding dress?"

"Well, I thought about doing it frontier-style, meaning

just wear calico and a veil, and I already have a calico dress. Poor girls on the frontier couldn't get wedding dresses and were married in whatever they had. But then I saw several wedding dresses in a collection in West Virginia, all from poor families, made of muslin with cheesecloth for the lace.''

"I saw those dresses with her," Ellen said. "They were beautiful, and muslin was readily available in Ohio in the 1860s. One was so well fitted the bride had to be sewn into it the morning of the wedding."

"Ooh, how erotic," Connie said. "You think the groom had to cut her out of the dress that night?"

"Guess so," Ellen said.

"Sexy."

"Ellen's going to help me," Amanda said. "We're going to have an authentic Appalachian wedding dress."

"Which means leave room for your swelling belly, right?" Connie said.

"No, for the zillionth time, I am *not* pregnant," Amanda said.

"Then why do we have to do all this in two months?" Molly said.

"Yes, Amanda, why does it have to be April? The weather would be more settled in May and there would be more flowers," Zenith said.

"Because—"

The front door opened. Amy Faron. "Sorry, couldn't leave the baby until my husband got home." Once again hugs and tears all around, except, once again, Bonnie didn't hug Amy. Or was it Amy who didn't hug Bonnie? Odd, Molly thought again. Very odd, indeed.

"What's this?" Amanda said, pointing to a winter bouquet in Amy's hands. "For me?"

"It was in front of the door," Amy said.

Amanda took it. "It's for you, Bonnie. There's a note here."

She handed it to her. Bonnie read the note and shrieked. Molly took the note.

"Bonnie, this is your last warning," it said.

TEN

BOUQUET

"I'LL GET JOHN," Molly said with a sigh.

John, Ken, and Briggs were down the hall in the kitchen. "How in hell did he slip up to the door and leave this?" Matins spluttered as he put the note in his wallet. "Did anybody else besides Amy come in the front door?" he asked the group.

"I did," Dawn said, "and I didn't see it."

"It would have been impossible to miss," Amy said. "It was leaning upright against the door."

"So sometime in the last two hours," Amanda said, "he must have slipped up and put it there because Dawn came about two and it's four now."

"In broad daylight. Can you imagine the nerve?" Connie said.

Zenith Wheeler came up, took the bouquet, and began identifying plants in it for Matins. Everything was winter foliage available just for the picking, she said—staghorn sumac heads, wild iris seed cases with their husks popped open like wooden petals, exploded milkweed pods, cattails, some hydrangea heads. "These hydrangea probably came from someone's yard; they don't grow wild. But everything else here could have come from the woods just outside."

"Look, he's tied it with honeysuckle vine," Amy said.

"Luke sure has style," Molly commented.

"He's damn bold, to come right up here and slip away

again,'' Matins was still fuming. ''What is he planning? State police don't know if he's armed or not. They thought not, but weren't sure. Can't believe he got by me.''

''Take it easy on yourself, Dad,'' Sherry said. ''You can't be everywhere at once. Beat up on Briggs, not on yourself.''

''Right,'' he said smiling slightly. ''Briggs, how could you let this happen?''

''Sorry, boss,'' Briggs said, and he laughed.

''Well, looks like we're here for a while longer,'' Matins said.

''No,'' Sherry said.

''What?''

''Well, if he's been to the door, he's seen you. Why don't you pretend to leave. I'll stay here and call you if needed.''

''Too dangerous.''

''We could leave the portable radio unit with her,'' Briggs said.

''Good idea,'' Matins said. ''We could put it in the kitchen and hide the patrol car down the road. You just punch the button and we'll be here in under thirty seconds. Think that'll work.''

Betty stepped in, and immediately they were silent. Sherry whispered in Molly's ear, ''We never tell Mom what our plans are; she'd freak.''

''Ah,'' Molly said, but she was thinking she was about to freak, too. She would be much more comfortable if they were sure Luke was unarmed. She would be even more comfortable if they weren't setting up this trap at all.

In the dining room, Florence, Bonnie, and Amanda had set up the buffet, and the women were filling up their plates. A trio of ornate antique porcelain teapots graced one end of the trestle table, each filled with hot water. An array of herbal teas lay beside them.

"Look, Bonnie," Amanda said. "Zenith brought some new tea blends."

"We had some here already, too. You can't be related to Zenith and not have some of her teas in the house."

"I buy your teas all the time," Mary-Mary said.

"Me too," added Connie. "They are the best, so invigorating."

"Thank you," Zenith said.

Ken had heaped a prodigious plateful of food, Matins and Briggs had more modest pileups.

"Dr. K, how do you stay so thin and eat like that?" Mary-Mary said.

"Must be all those studies he reads; it burns calories," Amanda said, giving him a hug. "What do you think of doing a reenactment for the wedding, Dad? It'd mean you'd have to dress in costume if you want to give away the bride."

"Yes, Dr. K," said Mary-Mary. "It's the oldest rule in reenacting. No one gets to dance unless they're dressed. No costume, no play."

"I like the idea. But how shall I dress? As a general?" Ken said.

"Maybe as a carpetbagger, Dad," Amanda suggested, not entirely kidding. Ken and Molly were technically newcomers to the Tricounty since they'd lived only fifteen years in the area. The carpetbagger idea had a certain cruel truth to it.

"I think I should dress as Lincoln," Ken said. "I'm tall enough and thin enough and I am from Illinois."

"Not accurate; he had no daughters," Amanda said.

"Accuracy is that important?"

"Accuracy is everything."

"Could I be a Confederate raider?"

"Yes, perfect, one of Morgan's men," Amanda said. "And easier, too, since Confederate uniforms were so irregular."

"Dr. K, will you be comfortable representing the Confederate view? That's part of reenacting, too, you have to explain to people not just costumes and things, but ideas, attitudes, what the people were fighting for," Dawn said.

"Actually, yes. I've been thinking a great deal about nineteenth-century attitudes recently," he replied.

"Why?" Amanda asked.

"I've been very puzzled by the resurgence of right-wing militia groups."

"Those crazies in the woods?"

"Unfortunately it may be more than a few gun-happy nuts playing in the woods. I'm beginning to think it's a genuine, if still fringe, movement, with a core of ideas, of norms. Mary-Mary, you took my classes, you should remember some of these terms."

"Not a one, Dr. K," she teased him.

"Yes, teaching is such a rewarding occupation." He sighed.

"But why do the militarists have you thinking about the Civil War?" Bonnie asked.

"I'm struck by the parallels. The ideas of militarist organizations bear a striking resemblance to those of the Confederacy."

"They're for slavery?" Dawn said, her lips curling in disgust.

"Well, there's much racism in the movement, you're right. But you have to remember that from the South's point of view the war wasn't about slavery, but about states' rights; in other words, about the seeming intrusion of the government in local affairs. Modern militarists tend to have extremely romanticized ideas of decentralized government. States' rights carried to almost getting rid of states. Conservative anarchy, if you can imagine such a thing. Like many extreme ideas, it has become attractive to hotheads, rowdies, and irresponsible charismatics. But underneath the madness, underneath any human madness actually, is always a core of ideas that can be traced historically. For better or worse, all ideas, no matter how dark or twisted they may seem to us, such ideas have roots in our culture. I think we can understand the paramilitary types by looking at the passions of the Civil War. Those ideas dispersed widely after the Civil War when veterans wandered West to Montana, Idaho, Arizona, New Mexico, California. And those ideas stayed here, too, as well, especially in our hill country, where there's less pressure for social change. Those ideas may be resurfacing in the paramilitary groups.''

"Oh my,'' Amanda said *sotto voce* to Molly. "Leave it to Dad to turn a bridal tea into a sociology class.''

"Would you like me to rescue your party, dear?'' Molly whispered back.

"Yes, Mom, please.''

"I will on one condition.''

"What's that?''

"Tell me why the wedding has to be in April.''

Amanda opened her eyes wide at the firmness in Molly's voice. Then she said, "Let's step out to the porch. I need your advice.''

Molly was deeply pleased; it was rare for Amanda to need her.

"Did you get along with your in-laws, with Grandma West?'' Amanda asked, leaning against the porch rail.

Ken's parents had both died before Amanda was two, which is why the question was in past tense.

"Yes and no," Molly said.

"What do you mean?"

"At first I felt the woman criticized everything I did, but in time she became a good friend. It happened when I decided her criticism was not reproach, but an effort to be friends. She didn't know how else to talk to a younger woman except by bossing her. When I pretended to listen, soon she quit criticizing."

"You became equals?"

"Sometimes it felt like it."

"Did she resent your taking Dad from her?"

"I don't know. Hard to say. He was her only son, so maybe. What does all this have to do with having the wedding in April?"

"Bently's mother is in Europe until then. This was his idea. She is the most awful person, Mom. She is so domineering, nothing ever pleases her. If you don't do things her way, she throws a tantrum. Bently figured the only way to have any fun with our wedding is to time it so it happens twenty-four hours after she returns. That way she can come, but she can't do much damage."

Molly laughed. "His parents are divorced?" she asked.

"Oh yes, and remarried. That's another reason for wanting a reenactment. Can you imagine the nightmare trying to figure out seating if we had a normal reception? We couldn't sit some of his family in the same room, let alone at the same table."

"Bently seems so easygoing," Molly said.

"It's a sculpted indifference, a shell to protect him from a zoo of a family."

"What makes you think weddings are supposed to be fun?" Molly said.

"They're not?"

"No, take it from me; they're to be endured. I can see why you want to avoid her and your timing it so close to her return will get you through the wedding, but not through your life. You don't marry a man, you marry a family. And if you exclude his mother from the wedding, she'll build up an insurmountable resentment. You'll never have any peace from her. Are you planning to live in Cleveland after the honeymoon?"

"Yes."

"And she lives up there, too?"

"Oh yes."

"Which means the mother you're used to quarreling with is a six-hour drive away, and the mother you have to learn to quarrel with is right in town. A bad strategy, I think, to start her off mad at you."

"It's Bently's idea."

"She'll blame you."

"I see your point. Do you think you and I are quarrelsome?" Amanda said.

Molly looked at her daughter, a puzzled frown on her face. Years of uproars flashed through her memory. "Peanut butter and jelly sandwiches?" she said softly.

Amanda laughed. "Surely you didn't think I was serious? I don't think I'll ever be able to joke with Bently's mother the way I do with you. If I had suggested peanut butter sandwiches to her for a wedding reception, she'd have thought I meant it."

It was a joke? Molly thought. Type A; Type B. How many times did she have to learn this lesson? Amanda had been "displaying" in that conversation. A display of anger from a Type A is not the same as a display from a Type B. Amanda was usually "talking things out" when she was fussing and fuming, even if Molly thought they were "arguing." Maybe theirs was a good relationship. After watching Bonnie and Florence together for a day, she knew she much preferred her relationship with her daughter to theirs.

"What do you think? It'll be hell on wheels if I put the wedding in May. She'll meddle us to death."

"But she'll be hell to live with afterward if you don't, right?"

"Right. I guess I have no choice. May it is. Horrors."

"What will she think of this Civil War scheme?"

"She'll hate it."

"And you think this wedding won't be fun? You don't think it won't be fun making her suffer?"

Amanda grinned. "You're right. I was thinking only about how *I* would suffer. But, yes, that's the attitude I need. If I approach this determined to enjoy every minute of her misery, I'll have fun."

"That's my girl."

Back in the parlor everyone had settled comfortably with their plates in front of the fireplace. Ken sat in a rocker, vigorously poking the logs to build the fire back up. Soon they were all discussing the May idea. The consensus was that May would mean better weather and that the extra time to promote the event would mean a better turnout.

"Besides," Molly commented, "in May all winter trail restrictions will be lifted in the National Forest, so you can have horses in the woods, a real cavalry charge, not just a show on the sidelines. And think of what will be in bloom then, lilacs, peonies, roses, rhododendrons, maybe iris, maybe you'll—" she heard Matins knocking at the door and turned to let him in, "—be able to get some dais—"

"Molly, don't open that door," Sherry yelled.

Too late, she already had. And it wasn't Matins at the door, but Luke.

ELEVEN

TEA

HE WAS SHIVERING, his hair wetly plastered to his skull. His orange prison jumpsuit was almost too muddy to still be called orange. He was wrapped in a blanket of some sort instead of wearing a jacket.

"May I come in, ma'am? I need to talk to Bonnie."

Molly stood there, too shocked to react. Sherry had ducked behind a couch and was now trying to crawl to the kitchen to punch the radio button.

"You poor child," Zenith said. "Here, give me that afghan," she said. She snatched it from a couch and brought it over to him. "Quick, Betty, get him a plate of food. And get him some herbal tea. Get something warm in him. Let's get him by the fire."

Zenith's commonsense fussing broke the tension. Luke, docile as a lamb, followed her to the fireplace and sat in Ken's rocker. Ken had stood and secreted a poker behind his back.

"Bonnie? Is she here? I got to talk to her," Luke mumbled.

Bonnie sat stone still on a couch between Amanda and Connie. He saw her there finally. "Bonnie, I've got somethin' to tell you. I've got to talk to you."

She didn't look at him.

"Please don't be afraid of me. I can't hurt you no more. I won't hurt nobody no more. I'm so sorry for the things I done. I didn't know how bad I hurt you until I heard you at that trial. I been thinking.''

"What're you doing here?" Bonnie hissed. "You know they'll just punish you more for escaping."

"You wouldn't come see me. You wouldn't answer my letters. I cain't blame you for that, so I had to come tell you I'm sorry."

"It'll wreck any chance you get for parole, you know that," Bonnie said.

"I ain't never going to get parole, Bonnie."

"Everybody gets paroled," Florence snapped. "That's why there's more bastards out of jail than in it."

"Please, Florence, it's Bonnie I got to talk to."

"Why?" Bonnie said.

"Bonnie, I'm real sick, some kind of cancer, something in the brain. It cain't be stopped. My dad died young, too. Maybe the same thing. I'm not going to live to parole, and I wanted to tell you before it was too late, that I'm sorry I hurt you. I ain't asking forgiveness. Chaplain said I need to atone, to be sorry, to try to make right all the bad things I done before I died, so here I am.''

Matins had stepped to the still-open door with Briggs beside him. Sherry had now edged to the fireplace, beside Ken.

Luke glanced up at the sheriff. "I kind of meant to tell just you alone like, but I see Sheriff Matins ain't going to give me time for a real private talk," he said.

"You really that sick?" Bonnie said.

"Been sick a long while, the doctor says. He thinks some of my rages might be lesions in the brain."

"Lesions?"

"Yeah, sores like. I've learnt lots of big words these last few months."

"I'm real sorry to hear you're so sick, Luke." Bonnie was studying her lap. Finally she looked up at him. "Thing I can't figure is, if you're so sorry, why'd you send me those threats?"

"What threats?"

"You know, the—gu—"

Matins interrupted. "No, Bonnie, let me handle this," he said. "How long have you been hanging about this house, Luke?" he said.

"Just got here. I was afraid to hitch. I walked the whole way, slept in barns. I just come out of those woods not more'n ten minutes ago."

"You were here sometime last night. We saw what you did."

"I swear, Sheriff, I ain't been here. I don't know what you're talking about."

Matins considered this for a minute. "Amanda, may I have a sheet of paper from your notebook?" He gave the paper to Luke. "Now write out, no I mean print out what you just said to Bonnie, about how sorry you are. Print her name on it." Luke frowned, but he did so, his hands still shaking from the cold.

Matins took the earlier note from his wallet and compared it with this new one. Molly peered over his shoulder. The letter strokes were nothing alike.

"Could be he's just cold and that'd change his hand," Matins said, more to himself than to his listeners.

"Somebody send this to Bonnie?" Luke said, his face twisting in surprise as he read the note.

Molly thought his surprise and shock were genuine, but Matins was skeptical.

"Yes," he said, "and we all think it was you. There were two other threats, too."

Luke looked at Bonnie, his mouth hanging open.

"Bonnie, I swear, as a man who believes, no, who knows, he's going to face his Maker real soon, that I never sent this. I wouldn't hurt you, Bonnie. I love you. I've always loved you."

Bonnie started to sob.

"Can I hug her?" Luke said to Matins. "Before you take me away?"

"Search him, Briggs."

"John, for God's sake, let him eat a hot meal before you take him," Betty said.

Matins rolled his eyes. "All right. Briggs, Sherry, take Luke and Bonnie to the kitchen, let them have a few minutes, not quite alone. Briggs and Sherry will have to stay with you, Luke, you understand? But I'll let you two talk a few minutes, and then we go, right?" They all walked down the servants' hall, Flo following.

"I'm going to call the warden, see if his story about being sick is true. Damn it; why didn't they tell me?" Matins said.

"Why?" Molly said.

"Don't you think that just might have given me a clue to his mental state? Bureaucrats. Damn them all." Then Matins, too, went into the kitchen, to use the phone. Betty and Molly exchanged glances.

"He's just mad at hisself for messing up," Betty said. "Luke should never even have gotten to the door, he thinks. He gets cranky when he's stupid."

"Ah," Molly said.

"Well, we can all relax now. Me, I'm going to have seconds," Ken said. "Mortal danger gives me an appetite. Who made these little pastries here? They're gr—" Another shriek. From the kitchen.

"This is the screamingest household," Amanda said. "Now what? Who screamed?"

"Me," Sherry hollered. "Hurry. Bonnie's fainted."

Zenith and Molly ran in, Amanda behind them. Bonnie lay on the floor, Matins and Luke kneeling beside her. Her face was clammy and pale, covered with a glistening sweat. Flo stood leaning on the table, shaking.

"If I didn't know better..." Zenith said, reaching for Bonnie's pulse. "Did she just drink something?"

"We were drinking this tea," Luke said.

"Don't touch those cups." Zenith had picked them both up and sniffed them. "Which one was Bonnie's?"

"This one."

Zenith took her wrist again. "Oh no, her pulse is fluttering. Quick, we'll have to make her vomit. Bonnie, honey, come to, we have to make you throw up. Come to, honey."

"Call an ambulance, Briggs," Matins said.

SOME HOURS LATER, Molly, Florence and Zenith, sat on the hard vinyl chairs outside the emergency room of the New Forge Hospital. It seemed to be a universal tradition that chairs outside hospital emergency rooms are always uncomfortable, Molly thought wearily. Bonnie was alive. Her stomach had been flushed; they'd followed with charcoal tablets to absorb the remaining poison. She'd also been hooked up to a heart monitor and was receiving saline IVs. Zenith's quick action to get the unabsorbed poison out of her stomach, plus Sherry's administering CPR, had probably saved her life, a nurse told them. Her heart may actually have stopped for a bit, she told them, although they couldn't be sure. The blood tests showed some digitalis in her system and maybe some alkaloids as well.

"Maybe foxglove for the digitalis," Zenith mused aloud to herself. "That's so potent even water from a vase of the flowers is dangerous. Only takes a few grams of foxglove to stop a heart. But where did the alkaloids come from? Aconite? Bloodroot? Daffodils? Hemlock? And how'd he get a hold of those things this time of year? He'd have to know where some were growing to dig up roots; that, or know where some dried roots were stored. Didn't know Luke was that smart.''

Things had been pure chaos at the mansion for a while. Molly remembered Sherry calmly putting the contents of both teacups into separate plastic refrigerator bins borrowed from Florence. John and Briggs had taken Luke and the plastic bins away. When the ambulance arrived there was more uproar while the cot was wheeled in. Molly vaguely remembered the other women milling about, Betty offering to take Ken and Pauline home, then Amanda herding her to a car to follow along to the hospital.

As for what everybody else did after that she really didn't know or care. People probably had just left. She was tired. And she felt betrayed. Luke had truly convinced her for a minute that he was penitent, and then he went and poisoned Bonnie like that. How could anyone be so evil, so devious? Her thoughts tumbled about in her head. Amanda leaned against the wall, looking as if she felt even worse.

''You okay, Amanda?'' Molly asked.

''Sitting here brings back bad memories, Mom, real bad,'' she said.''

''For me, too,'' Molly said.

Another nurse stepped out. ''We've decided to admit her, to keep her overnight for observation. She's awake, if you want to see her, but just for a minute. She's very weak.''

''Is she going to be all right?'' Amanda asked.

"The doctor thinks so, yes. But she'll need fluids, and we want to watch her heartbeat, too."

As they stepped in, Bonnie smiled a little. "Hi, Mom," she said. "Some party." Flo just shook her head.

"You're one lucky girl," Amanda said. "If Zenith hadn't been there..."

"Thanks, Aunt Zenith. You're the best."

Molly felt a presence behind her. She turned. Matins.

"Hi, kid," he said to Bonnie. "You do like to scare people. I think I got twelve new gray hairs tonight."

Bonnie smiled wanly.

"Course those were the only ones I had left that weren't gray." Bonnie almost laughed. The nurse signaled for them to leave.

"Zenith, Florence, you have rides home?" Molly said.

"I'll take Florence home," Zenith said. "Good night."

"You too. John, good night," Molly said.

"A moment, Molly," he said.

He waited until Zenith and Florence had turned down the hall. "You two, are you too tired to talk to me?"

"Yes," Molly said.

"Tough. I need to talk to you both. Let's go sit in the cafeteria."

When they'd settled around a table, he sat a minute, stirring his coffee. Finally, he said, "All right, Molly, tell me everything you remember."

"From when?"

"From the minute that stupid toy gun arrived. If anybody's going to have noticed something little, it's you, Molly. So just start thinking. Everything."

"Uh, isn't this an open-and-shut case?" Molly said. "Luke escapes from jail, poisons Bonnie, end of case?"

"No, I wish. I like open-and-shut cases."

"You believe his repentance story?"

"Yes. Now don't let it get about a sheriff believes a felon, but I really believe him."

"Haven't we got this relationship backwards? I'm supposed to be the outraged busybody who knows the cops have the wrong man. And you're supposed to be the stubborn, arrogant detective who can't appreciate my wisdom," Molly said. Amanda grinned, but said nothing.

"I know, I know," Matins said. "People are going to say I'm daft. But I believe his story. The warden said he was really sick, terminal, just like he said. In fact, he said it was amazing Luke had the physical strength to get here. He's bad off. Must have been going on pure will. So humor me. Think."

Molly looked at Amanda. Amanda shrugged.

"Was that gun thing just this morning? Seems like weeks ago," Molly said.

"What sorts of things should we try to remember?" Amanda asked.

"Anything. Who might have reason to be mad at Bonnie. Who might be knowledgeable about herbs and poisons. Who arrived with whom. Who talked about what. Who brought what. Who sat with who?"

"Or who didn't sit with whom?" Molly asked.

Matins smiled slowly. "Perfect. Yeah. Who wouldn't sit with somebody."

"Bonnie didn't hug Dawn and Amy."

"That's crazy," Amanda said. "Just crazy. Neither woman could hurt anyone or have anything against Bonnie, although Amy might have some knowledge of herbs. She poses as a herbalist sometimes at reenactments."

"No one knows as much about herbs as Zenith, though," Molly said.

"And Bonnie'd be dead right now if she didn't know what she knows," Amanda rejoined.

"Let's say Amy brought the flowers, instead of just finding them. She could have assembled the bouquet," Matins said.

"Or Dawn could have put it there and no one found it until Amy arrived," Molly said.

"All right, let's start with Dawn. Tell me about Dawn. Why might Bonnie not like Dawn?"

"Dawn's just quiet," Amanda said. "If she's not speaking, it doesn't mean she's mad."

"Speculate. Could they dislike each other?"

"Dawn once said she thought Bonnie ought to get in some cosmetics for blacks, but if Dawn's got a beef, she says it," Amanda said. "She said that right out to Bonnie. I think if there's any tension, it's the other way around. Bonnie's a little awkward around Dawn, like a lot of whites, just a little too polite to her. Maybe Bonnie feels it might be impolite to remind Dawn she's descended from slaves, which is silly. Dawn's proud of her heritage. But what black person isn't aware when a white person is just too polite? Dawn might just be reacting to Bonnie's stiffness."

"Are you and Dawn close enough to talk to each other this bluntly?" Molly said to Amanda.

"Oh yes. She has a fantastic sense of humor. It's fun to get her talking about customers who come into the shoe outlet at the factory and think she gives shines instead of owning the place."

"Interesting friendship," Molly said.

"Very, but humor is how she deals with people like Bonnie, not hostility."

"What about Amy, then?" Matins said.

"Amy we know only through the Damn Yankees. She

joined after reading in the paper about one of our Labor Day demonstrations. She likes to wear those long dresses and cook beans over an open fire. She says it lets her pretend she's her great-great-great-grandmother who came over from Germany in the 1840s as a bride to a foundry worker. Amy's cool. She makes a small living out of her home by running a coupon school. For a fee, she teaches women how to save sixty, seventy, eighty dollars a month by using coupons."

"I should take her course," Molly said.

"You may have trouble getting a spot. She was recently featured in a newspaper article, so she has lots of students right now. She has a new baby, about four months old. Her husband, Dwight Faron, is a truck mechanic, works on the big rigs for a shipping company down by Portsmouth. I can't think of a single link she has to Bonnie except for the club."

"What do you know about her family?" Matins said.

"Not much. Her own parents are just folks; her in-laws are divorced. She and Dwight just got back from a visit to his mother in the Southwest, but his father is still in the area, lives with Dwight's grandmother."

"Okay," Matins said. "Let's assume one of the other women put it there sometime between Dawn's arrival and Amy's. So do any others in that room have reason to dislike Bonnie?"

Amanda shrugged.

"Who else was there?"

"Lorraine?" Molly prompted.

"I don't like this, Mom. These women are my friends, have been since I was ten."

"If someone tried murder, this someone needs help, Amanda," Molly said softly.

"Okay. Lorraine used to date Luke in high school, but

I think she's relieved to have lost him to Bonnie, not angry

about it.''

"Lorraine who?" Matins said.

"Lorraine DeWitt."

"Connie?" Molly again prompted.

"Connie Tanton," Amanda said with a wooden tone. She faced Matins who was now taking notes. "Connie's ex-husband has dated Bonnie a few times. I know that troubles her. It's his right; they are separated. But it troubles her. But that's no motive."

"His name?" Matins said.

"Brice. Brice Fremantle."

"Mary-Mary?" This from Molly.

"Mary-Mary O'Dell. Again, like Amy, she's just someone we know through the club."

"Ellen?"

"Ellen McKnight. Same."

"Sherry?" Matins said, though he winced as he said it.

Amanda put a hand on his arm. "Not even remotely possible. Until today, I don't think she even knew Bonnie. Remember, she is enough older than me that she didn't play with my friends. More like someone I knew because our parents, you guys, were good friends. She was always like an older sister, someone who'd tell you about sex and makeup, but was never a playmate."

"It can't be Jennifer St. Johns; she didn't come," Molly said.

"Actually, if anyone has a motive, it's her," Amanda said. "While she was on maternity leave, she lost her job as cosmetics consultant at the store."

"To Bonnie?" Matins said.

"Yes."

"Don't you think these are trivial things, John? Like soap-opera hostilities? Don't you think they're too trivial a basis for attempted murder?" Molly said.

"Yes, I do," he said. "Extremely trivial."

"Could there be a link between this poisoning attempt and the body in the cave?"

"That's way far-fetched, Molly," Matins said.

"Not really. Think about it. Bonnie and Florence live in a house over a murdered body that the murderer or murderers don't want found. So maybe the murderer decides to get rid of both of them and use Luke's escape as cover, to try to make it look like Luke did the killing."

"Now you're as daft as I am. Besides, we don't know if the body was murdered yet. Or human."

"Nice talking to you, John. Amanda and I are tired and are going home. By the way, is Ken a suspect?"

"No, of course not."

"Then every one of your suspects is a woman," Molly said.

"Well, well, well," Matins said thoughtfully. "All women. That's something new for sure."

" 'Night, John."

They left him still brooding over his coffee cup.

PART THREE

SOMETHING BORROWED

TWELVE

WWW.COM

MAY HAD NEVER BEEN lovelier, Molly thought as she stocked her van for the day's run. Now all she had to do was somehow survive the month. The wedding/reenactment was one week away and plans for it were coming along fine, although, once again, not as she had expected.

For one thing, she had been surprised by Ken's enthusiasm. He was becoming more of a reenactment fanatic than Amanda. He had read a dozen books on the Civil War, visited half a dozen regional museums, including two in Kentucky, and surfed the Web for hours to learn all he could about the Confederacy and reenacting. His costume was growing piece by piece in one of their closets. He had decided to be a rough, illiterate, barely disciplined infantry fighter from "Old Kaintuck," complete with tattered uniform, bad shoes, slouch hat, scruffy beard, fake accent, and "a taste fer homemade likker. A'gwin t'carry it rat in this beat-up ol' canteen which'n I took off'n sum po' Yankee bastid."

"You wouldn't, would you?" Molly had replied to that idea.

"Wouldn't I though?" he'd said, his eyes twinkling.

"And shouldn't it be 'this *here* beat-up canteen?'" she'd criticized.

For a second thing, she'd been surprised that, despite Amanda's portrayal of her, Bently's mother, Maria Jane

Bently Cottingham Bellamy, had turned out to be something less than an ogre. In fact, Molly concluded, Maria Jane was no more bossy than Amanda.

Maria Jane, after a few vain attempts to enlist Molly in a protest against the reenactment idea, had reversed strategies and decided to endorse it wholeheartedly, to be more committed than either Amanda or Bently. While Molly was going as the famous but prim nurse, Clara Barton, Maria Jane chose to be a saloon girl. She wanted to be the most provocative saloon girl ever, she told Molly, but couldn't find the bustier or the garters. Then Ken found a supplier on one of his Web surfs. Molly gave Maria Jane the address, and it cemented a real friendship.

The bridesmaids each selected an area of responsibility. Ellen McKnight, of course, was making the dress. Sherry Matins was cordoning off the viewing area for civilian spectators, marking the assembly sites for Union and Confederate units, and seeing that all regulations for public events, such as police and ambulance support, were taken care of. Lorraine DeWitt was handling negotiations with the National Forest and the Division of Natural Resources for appropriate permits, a cruel assignment given her phone phobia, but she'd laughed as she promised not to be too neurotic about it, at least until after the wedding.

Dawn Cannon, Amanda said, as the owner and manager of one of the larger businesses in the Tricounty, was a natural logistician, so her assignment was to organize the crafts demonstrations. Thus far, Dawn had found a soap maker, a moonshiner, a storyteller, a carpenter who used period tools, a blacksmith, and a barber/dentist. "He has a collection of authentic instruments, not reproductions, but originals," she had crowed to Molly in a phone report a few days ago.

"Is he a real dentist?" Molly had asked.

"Oh no, he's a high-school football coach, so he doesn't work on teeth at reenactments, but he says he frequently gives soldiers and even spectators shaves. He charges a quarter for a clean shave, fifty cents for beards."

"Isn't that high for the nineteenth century?"

Dawn had laughed. "I said the same thing, and he said, 'Hey, this is war.' "

Bonnie Siever, now fully recovered from the poisoning, was cleaning and decorating an abandoned log cabin in the woods which Dawn had told them about. It was about a quarter mile off the hiking trail and would make a good site for the battle, the wedding, and the ball because there was a clearing in front. The cabin didn't have a floor, but the roof was sound; it was safe, Dawn had said. Her church used the cabin as their gathering point for the annual February march to honor Zachariah Williams.

Bonnie was also to gather all the flowers the day of the wedding. At the moment she had calls out to neighbors and friends asking them to watch for nice rhododendron and lilac shrubs in bloom.

Mary-Mary O'Dell was arranging for music and musicians for both the wedding and the ball and had found an authentic brass quintet; all the players were from West Virginia. Molly didn't react to that last detail so Mary-Mary explained. "West Virginia, don't you see? That means they can play like the very devil." Molly assumed that was a compliment.

Jennifer St. Johns was collecting firewood for the campers and the bonfires at the ball.

Amy Faron was persuading her father-in-law, Samuel Faron, to bring his team of draft horses and wagon to give rides to the children and to haul guests up to the mansion for the reception.

And Connie Tanton was doing the registrations. All reenactment participants had to register and pay a small fee to participate, she explained to Molly, plus sign a waiver exempting event organizers—"that's us"—of liability in case of injuries during the battle.

"I thought Amanda said the event was free," Molly said.

"To spectators, yes, but wood, food, straw—someone has to pay for those things. They can register the day of the event, but we told them they'd get prime campsites and roles if they register beforehand," she'd explained.

"Roles?"

"You know, who gets to be Union or Confederate or infantry or artillery and such."

"Or cavalry?"

"Nah, if you show up with a horse, you're cavalry. Nobody argues. Mounted troops are a rare treat. The reenactment of Morgan's capture at Buffington Island last summer was supposed to be on horseback, but only two horses showed up. Great horses though, beautifully trained."

Molly's job, naturally, inevitably, as mother of the bride, was to be phone central, with Ken as backup e-mail central. By now Molly had become well acquainted with the phone voices of all the bridesmaids and of Kevin Logan, the quartermaster of the Ohio 92nd. "Our unit owns four wall tents," he announced in one of his calls. "We'll use one for a field hospital. You can do your nursing demonstrations there. Think you can show how to roll bandages and wrap wounds by then?"

"I think so. What's a wall tent?"

"One you can stand up in."

"Oh."

"Also we should set up a water supply at the hospital tent; reenacting is hot work. Two of the other tents are for company headquarters, one for each side, and the fourth can be a hotel. Anyone who wants to be a lady of ill repute can hang out there."

"What about the soldiers? Amanda says most will be in camp by Friday night."

"They'll bring their own tents, or some are such sticklers for accuracy they'll sleep on the ground. But we will need some straw for bedding. Do you know a local supplier?"

Zenith had a barn filled with straw and, when asked about it, offered to lend it. The reenactors could return any intact bales, although she would have to charge for any they broke, she'd said apologetically.

Molly had laughed. "This is the first wedding I ever heard of where the 'something borrowed' will be straw."

Ken and John had been taking turns mowing the cabin clearing in hopes that it would be more like a lawn and less like a thistle patch by the day of the wedding. The plan was for the Confederacy and Union to move from separate assembly points toward the cabin, have their battle in the clearing, and then, when it was ended, mingle to serve as honor guard for the bride and groom. Since the couple had been Union when they met, it was decided the Union could win the day this time.

After the ceremony, everyone would break for dinner. The immediate wedding party would go to the Barton Mansion for a buffet, the rest to be at the mercy of sutlers or their own picnic baskets. Then would follow the ball, complete with period tunes, and, Kevin promised, "We have some ladies coming all the way from Kentucky who can teach you newcomers the waltzes.''

The wedding dress was proceeding just as beautifully. The bleached muslin seemed from a distance almost white and was worked into a three-tiered skirt to fit over hoops. A separate shirred bodice with leg-of-mutton sleeves completed the dress. Molly had been surprised to learn that most Victorian-era dresses were in two pieces, separate bodice and skirt. Amanda had told her that her first dress had been wrong because her bodice had not matched her skirt. ''Everyone was so polite. No one told me it was wrong until I asked. But once I asked, man, did I get an earful about Victorian dress design.'' Now she always did it right, she said, two pieces, both matching.

Amanda was coming in for a final fitting tonight. Molly had asked Ellen to keep the veil Louella and her friends were making a secret. She wanted it to be a surprise, a wedding present for Amanda.

Wedding presents. Amanda and Maria Jane had quarreled about those at length at first. Maria Jane, accustomed to the wealth of all three of her families, the Bentlys, Cottinghams, and Bellamys, wanted Amanda to register at a posh department store in Cleveland. Amanda, mindful of her Appalachian friends' more limited means, wanted to be listed at Formby's, the hardware store in New Forge.

Molly suggested a compromise. The couple had lived together three years. They already had china, a four-slice toaster, embroidered towels, and a high-torque cordless screwdriver. There was nothing they needed, so why not solicit donations for the Damn Yankees Club instead? Amanda thought that was a terrific idea and put the request out over the Web on her home page.

That home page, what a marvelous tool, Molly decided. Everyone who had a modem knew instantly what was going on. That Web site was why things were going so smoothly, she was sure. Amanda had worked up some Civil War-era graphics in hypertext markup language (known to insiders as html) and she'd set up the hypertext transfer protocols (or http://). Ken maintained the page. Every morning, he updated any information and replied to a flurry of messages. They were getting queries from as far away as Virginia and Indiana about the reenactment, he said.

Everything for the wedding, it seemed, was coming together perfectly.

Coming along less perfectly, however, were any developments on any of Matins's three investigations. He'd not been able to uncover any more information about Bonnie's poisoner; in fact he was beginning to think it all had been just a bad batch of tea, that Zenith might have mixed up her supplies of ingredients and accidentally put some dangerous stuff in one of the mixes. Of the threats, he was starting to think Luke had to have made them, after all.

He had learned from the OSU anthropology professor that, yes, the remains in the tunnel had been human—specifically, white, male, about forty-five—and had died within the last ten years. A check of dental records suggested that the body was, as he suspected, probably David Wheeler. But cause of death could not be determined. The anthropologist said the person could have died where he lay and only been lightly covered with soil. But he could find no bullet rip or knife scratches on any of the bones. There were no hair or nail tissues left for chemical analysis, and even if there had been, the acidity of the soil would have distorted the results, he'd said. The body did seem to have been tied at the wrists when it died, judging by the placement of the bones, but the killers must have used cotton cord or sisal twine, rather than nylon, for the rope to disappear so thoroughly, he'd suggested.

If it was Wheeler, Matins had no idea who might have done it or why. Bonnie and Florence took the news fairly calmly when he'd told them. Both felt David could have had enemies, given his temperament, but since he had rarely told either of them where he went or who he had been with, they couldn't say who'd want to kill him. Florence said that, in a strange way, it was a relief to realize he hadn't left her, that whoever left the note did it to make her and Matins believe he was alive.

As for Matins, he was furious at himself for not suspecting a murder when David Wheeler disappeared. "The only detective-type thing I did in that case," he told Molly, "was check to be sure the handwriting on the note was different from Florence's when she wrote her statement. I mean, it was so like David to pull a stunt like this, that I didn't suspect. It's as if someone were using my knowledge of local people against me."

"John, you mustn't take this so personally," Molly said.

"I know, Molly. But a six-year-old murder? How in the hell am I going to even begin to solve it?"

Also not going well during these past two months were Matins's and Louella's attempts to learn if a gun smuggler were operating in the Tricounty. The Tricounty Old Ladies Network had met weekly since March to work on Amanda's veil, but Louella said there was nothing in the gossip that she felt had anything to do with gun smugglers or paramilitarists.

The ladies were meeting that afternoon to complete

assembly of the wedding veil. Louella was sure Molly would be able to surprise Amanda with it when she came in tonight for her fitting—on one condition, Louella had said, waggling a finger at her. "I get to be thar t'see the look on her face when you give it t'her."

Molly had laughed. "Of course."

Delivering a dozen meals to one house was easy for the Meal Van. Zenith and Betty were taking care of driving the old women to Louella's for the weekly crochet and gab session. Molly then followed with the meals. The women were all old-time Tricounty natives and each had relatives who had done something in the Civil War, not necessarily an honorable something, but at least something. To a one, they were thrilled by the reenactment; each was planning to come, in costume, and, if possible, dressed as someone from her family history.

They were intimidating, these women. Singly, each was a handful; in a group, they were a tidal force. Molly took a deep breath, turned the key in the van, and started the drive to Louella's.

THIRTEEN

HOOKS

USUALLY the old women were sitting in Louella's tiny living room crocheting when Molly arrived with the food. But today, with assembly of the strips the scheduled project, they were standing or sitting around the kitchen table. Strips were laid on this table, and the women excitedly debated the arrangement. Molly gasped at their beauty. It was the first she'd seen all the squares together. Each woman had a specialty stitch, unique to her, in some cases unique to her family for generations. There were rosettes and butterflies, shells and cascades, lattices and fence rows—at least these are what their crafters called them, but they were lace, utter lace, airy as a dream, all made from a frail white twine that snapped at a tug, but when worked, was as strong as rope.

"Molly, you crying?" Louella said, surprised.

"They're beautiful."

"We can't agree here," Louella said. "Bridget thinks Edna's star stitch should be the first row, but Alyce here says the snapdragon is prettier. What do you think, Molly?"

"They're both pretty," Pansy interjected hurriedly. "It's just that the first row is the one to be pinned to her hair, it's gotta take the weight of the veil and the stress of the pins. The star stitch is heftier, more stable, don't you think so, Bertha?"

Bertha stood, obviously torn with indecision. Molly

thought it all looked too delicate to be even breathed on, but Louella had assured her the veil could last centuries if Amanda kept it out of sunlight and lying flat in a box. Crochet was tough. How could Louella be so confident? Molly had asked, and Louella had shown her her own wedding veil that a great-grandmother had made just before the Civil War. Louella had had only boys and so far only grandsons, so she was hoping for a great-granddaughter to give it to.

Molly left the women still feverishly discussing and went to set up the meals, a dozen today, counting herself, since she planned to stay and wait for Amanda. Ken was instructed to bring Amanda over to Louella's as soon as she arrived, but not to tell her anything.

Pansy Chalmers and Bertha Benton Connors Ford were regulars, Louella had explained to Molly after one of these crochet sessions—that is, they were always invited to any gathering of the Tricounty Old Lady Network, no matter what its purpose. In fact, they were the only ones who knew that this was Louella's term for the get-tos. The other women just thought they'd received "a social invite."

Charlotte Bannich was an almost regular, that is, she was usually invited, but not always. Louella had not explained what the criteria were for inviting her, and Molly knew better than to ask a direct question by now. All the other women were selected especially for this assignment, either for their crochet skills or because Louella thought they might have knowledge of activities of some of the more sinister of the Tricounty's men, though of course Louella didn't tell even her regulars about that second objective.

These seven were: Alyce Wheeler, mother of Robert and the late David Wheeler; Edna Faron, Amy Faron's grand-mother-in-law; Bridget Tanton, Connie Tanton's grandmother; Patricia Siever, Luke Siever's grandmother; Katrin Wilton-Jones, mother of a local radio personality; Mary Smith, one of Mary-Mary O'Dell's grandmothers; and Mary O'Dell, Mary-Mary's other grandmother. Molly wondered how Louella got those last two to agree to sit in the same room, let alone work together. And she smiled to think there was an Edna in the group. Edna was the Jennifer of the sixty-plus set. There were always one or two Ednas present. All the women came every time; they seemed to regard a request from Louella as a command.

Molly didn't always have time to sit and listen to the conversations over these past weeks, but she'd done so often enough to hear each woman's Civil War stories. Louella had started the tale-telling several weeks ago simply by announcing that an ancestral uncle had been an aide to Brigadier General John Beatty, the famous diarist. This uncle had even taken dictation of some entries when the general was too tired to write for himself.

Pansy Chalmers immediately was able to top that story. She was descended from a Virginia Dougherty nicknamed Hard-Luck because he'd lost all his property, including slaves, at gambling. He'd drifted into Pennsylvania and either joined or was drafted by the Union army. Almost immediately two-thirds of his company were captured in a skirmish in Virginia because he had the hard luck to be led by an incompetent colonel. Then, because the Confederacy didn't have facilities to build prisons, poor Hard-Luck had been held on a swampy, mosquito-infested sandspit in the middle of a river. One night the river started to rise and Hard-Luck got lucky for a change. He snagged a passing tree trunk and floated to freedom.

Bertha Benton Connors Ford's story was about the first black infantry units that had been organized out of Cincinnati in 1862. Some had been trained by a grandfather of one of her husbands. She had later brought a letter from him to show the group, and she'd let Molly copy them for Dawn. One paragraph in particular shocked Molly deeply:

I have got relieved of my 'nigger' command, and right glad I am, too. But I must say that they learn the drill as fast as any soldiers, for they know nothing but pay attention and obey orders. They appear to become very much attached to their officers, will follow them anywhere & do anything for them, & they will fight.

"How typical of the times," Louella had said. Another letter from the same ancestor to a brother said:

I have no objection to them [lacks] being soldiers. Wish the President would draft every able-bodied one North and South. There is not a Negro in the army that is not a better man than a rebel to this government.... No traitor is too good to be killed by a Negro.

When Molly gave the copies of the letters to Dawn a few days later, she had said, "Well, at least someone was lower than an African-American in this man's view."

Dawn had laughed. "It's scary how blunt history is. I think that's what I like about reenacting—it gives us all a way to talk frankly about race or gender or class prejudices without getting personal."

At every session, Louella's crochet group was brimful

of Civil War stories. Charlotte Bannich said one of her
ancestors had marched with Sherman to the sea, but she
didn't know much more than that. Alyce Wheeler had
gasped in mock horror because, she said, one of her ancestors had been burned out by Sherman's sweep. "Yer
ancester prob'ly raped my gran'ma. Mebbe we're more
related than y'think," she'd said. The group had giggled
wildly at that notion, and Molly was shocked that these
prim old ladies could be so earthy.

Patricia Siever told of her great-great-aunt who had
been a Union sympathizer living in the Deep South.
There was no one she could talk to about her feelings,
so she had kept a diary until she ran out of paper in 1863.
The Sievers still had the diary in the family and would
Molly like to see it, she'd asked, pretending to be shy,
but in truth wanting very much to outdo Bertha Benton
Connors Ford's coup with the letters. Molly was chilled
by some of that poor woman's entries:

New Orleans, Dec. 1 1860. I understand it now.
Keeping journals is for those who cannot, or dare
not, speak out.

Jan 26, 1861. The solemn boom of cannon today
announced that the convention have passed the or-
dinance of secession.

April 20, 1861. Edith said come help me dress her
negro Chloe. Chloe is a recent purchase from Geor-
gia. There is a ball tonight in aristocratic colored
society and Henry is taking her. We superintended
Chloe's very stylish toilet and then Edith said, run
into your room please and write a pass for Henry.
But Henry is free, I said. That makes no difference,

said Edith. All colored people must have a pass if out late.

May 10. Today I was pressed into service to make red flannel cartridge-bags. I basted while Mrs. S sewed, and I felt ashamed to think that I had not the moral courage to say, "I don't approve of your war and won't help you, particularly in the murderous part of it."

Sept. 25. When I opened the door of Mrs. F's room on my return the rattle of two sewing machines and a blaze of color met me. "Ah, G. you are just in time to help us: these are coats for Jeff Thompson's men. All the cloth in the city is exhausted; these flannel lined oil-cloth tablecovers are all we could obtain to make overcoats. They will be very warm and serviceable." Serviceable—yes! The Federal army will fly when they see those coats! the most bewildering combination of brilliant, intense reds, greens, yellows and blues in big flowers meandering over as vivid grounds; and as no tablecover was large enough to make a coat, the sleeves of each were of a different color and pattern.

Jackson. Oct. 26, 1862. All the world appears to be traveling through Jackson. There were many refugees from New Orleans, among them acquaintances of mine. The peculiar styles of dress necessitated by the exigencies of war gave the crowd a very striking appearance. In single suits I saw sleeves of one color, the waist of another, the skirt of another.

Oak Haven. Oct. 31, 1862. Mr. W. said last night

the farmers felt uneasy about the "Emancipation
Proclamation" to take effect in December. The
slaves have found it out, though it had been carefully kept from them. "Do yours know it?" I asked.
"Oh, yes, Finding it to be known elsewhere, I told
it to mine with fair warning what to expect if they
tried to run away. The hounds are not far off."

Vicksburg, April 28, 1863. I never understood before
the full force of those questions—what shall we eat?
What shall we drink? And wherewithal shall we be
clothed...? Making shoes is now another accom-
plishment. Mine were in tatters. H. came across a
moth-eaten pair that he bought me, giving ten dollars I think. And they fell into rags when I tried to
wear them; but the soles were good. A pair of old
coat sleeves—nothing is thrown away now—was in
my trunk and I cut an exact pattern from my old
shoes, and sewed the cloth to the soles. I am so
proud of these home-made shoes, think I'll put them
in a glass case when the war is over, as an heirloom.

Friday June 5, in the cellar. It is our custom in the
evening to sit in the front room a little while in the
dark and watch the shells. H. suddenly sprang up,
crying *Run!* Where? *Back.* I started through the back
room, H. after me. I was just within the door when
the crash came that threw me to the floor. It was the
most appalling sensation I'd ever known—worse
than an earthquake which I've also experienced.
Shaken and deafened, I picked myself up. We lit a
candle to see, then found the entire side of the front
room torn out.

When Molly had finished reading, she had excused herself from the group to walk a while by Louella's house. Before this day, the Civil War had been a couple of chapters in a college history book, a few memorized dates, a few names of generals. But when seen as women see it, it was changed for her to something vivid, real. She walked until she reached the lip of the ridge and could look out over the valley. The dogwoods were in full bloom, their ultrawhite bracts glistening randomly among the early mixed greens of the trees below.

Most Northern soldiers would never have seen the dogwoods like this until they went into the South for war. They must have commented in their letters on the paradox of so much beauty in the midst of so much death. Morgan's invaders had slipped through those dogwoods below. Terror had filled that valley beneath her, but the terror was not only of the raiders. How many had kept journals because they could not trust their neighbors? One family in that valley below would be for the South, one for the Union. One would help a bounty hunter, one would help the fleeing slaves. Betrayals from that time must still be festering in some of those families below.

"Tell me," she'd asked Amanda a few days later when her daughter was down on one of her many working visits, "what first sparked your interest in the Civil War?"

"Oh, I don't know. It was something everyone around here had in common, no matter what their background. North, South, rich, poor, every family had a Civil War story. It was a way to get my many different friends to like each other. As for me, I felt our family didn't have a past. Since the Civil War is the defining event in American history, it must be part of our past even if I didn't know how.''

''That doesn't really explain your interest, though.''

''I think what it gives me, besides lots of friends and an excuse to go camping, was something for me and Dad to talk about. He loved the stories. It was one of the few topics where he'd listen and I'd talk instead of the other way around.''

''I see.''

After reading that diary, Molly made two decisions—one, to rework her costume so none of the pieces matched, sleeves, bodice, or skirt. And two, to make Ken a wild oilcloth coat, as a surprise. He would love it. And he would wear it, too.

She had thought nothing could top the Siever diary, but at the very next session of the Tricounty Old Lady Network, Bridget Tanton took a turn, prefacing her story by saying she was almost embarrassed to tell of her ancestor, since he never did anything but guard the railroads, although since Morgan and his men liked to burn them out all the time, it wasn't completely hazard-free. It wasn't like saying you had someone at Vicksburg, she'd said with a pointed glance at Patricia, but it had its moments.

Seeing that glance, Molly for the first time understood that the storytelling was a competition. It was also the first she understood Louella's information-gathering technique. Louella never asked questions; she just told a story and waited for her listeners to tell better ones in hopes, almost a certainty in Appalachian circles, that they would tell too much.

Bridget, after a dramatic pause, followed with an equally dramatic thrust of her hand into her crochet bag and pulled out a letter carefully encased in stiff plastic.

The letter told the recipient of the sender's regret at having to inform the family of the death of one Hiram Tanton, who died valiantly in action near Murfreesboro and whose last words were "Bury me where I have fell." The letter praised the young man as "a hero of heroes, noted for reckless daring and universally beloved."

"How sad," Molly had said when Bridget finished reading the letter. Bridget had snorted. The letter was a fake. The real author was this selfsame Hiram Tanton. He was angry because his family was lazy about answering his letters and he decided he would write a letter "that would get their damned attention. An' it did. They put up a stone an' everything before learning the truth."

Katrin Wilton-Jones submitted her tale-topping entry next, about a Virginia ancestor, a Confederate officer, who went into South Carolina and courted a wealthy heiress. He succeeded, too, and rapidly, since the war made women willing. The young woman bewitched by his dashing glamour and besotted with love for him of course agreed that he should handle all her business interests. Soon after they were married he had to go on a short business trip to Virginia and suggested the two lovebirds drink to each other's health before he left. The wine was poured, but then the man was called to the door by a sudden caller. Mooning over the coming parting, the young bride took a sip from his glass where his lips had touched and then put her own glass in its place. They drank and within an hour he took ill and died. In deep grief, she traveled to Virginia to meet and mourn with his family, where she discovered that he already had a wife and several children. It was only then she realized the glass had been poisoned and intended for her. "But if he hadn'ta had those children by his furst wife, I couldn't be tellin' you today what a bastard he ware,"

Katrin concluded, again to much laughter from the other women.

Mary Smith took her turn, boasting that a way-back cousin, George Eastin, rode with Morgan. That brought a gasp of admiration from all the women, including Molly.

"He ware a romantic sort, too, almost too romantic," Mary said. She explained that he and some friends were dinner guests of several young Kentucky ladies. All were discussing the crimes of a Union Colonel Haisley, who was thought to have told his soldiers that any Southern woman who showed contempt for Union soldiers would be treated as a common prostitute.

One of the younger belles jumped to her feet and said, "I will marry any Confederate soldier who kills the tyrant Haisley."

Eastin said, "I accept the challenge, miss."

"Well soldiers bein' soldiers," Mary spun out her tale, "he forgot his promise in about ten minutes. Now that night as the three were gallopin' back to Morgan's camp they were overtaken by three Federal cavalry, one of whom was none other than the notorious Colonel Haisley, but my cousin didn't know it then. All he knowd was he had some feisty Yankee a'chasing and a'shootin' him. It was a chase and a fight the like of which you never saw. Then the Yankee Haisley was unhorsed. My cousin Eastin demanded he surrender. Haisley put up his hands. When Eastin come up to take his weapon, Haisley shot him, but missed. Eastin was so stunned by the man's cheatin' he just stuck his own pistol to Haisley's head and shot him dead.

"Only then did one of them other Yankees inform my cousin that he had shot the dread Colonel Haisley. Eastin then remembers his promise to that young lady, only see, he didn't want to marry her at all and he didn't know what to do. He thought about running, but that'd just get him a court-martial so he asked his commanding officer to go speak to her. Turns out she didn't want to marry him any more'n he wanted to marry her, so it worked out, but I think he was a little more careful about promising marriages after that.''

Mary O'Dell turned, maybe for the first time since the wedding-veil group had been meeting, to speak directly to Mary Smith and smiled with anticipated triumph. ''Your damn cousin is the bastard who killed my great-uncle Haisley, but he lied. He shot Haisley after he'd surrendered. And Haisley never issued any such order about women; that was a damned Rebel lie.''

''Not true,'' Mary said.

''True, true, true,'' the other Mary said.

''That's why they hate each other, they's mad about something that happened a hunnert-thirty some odd years ago,'' Pansy whispered none too softly to Molly.

The only woman not to have told a tale yet these weeks was Edna Faron.

Louella decided to prompt her a little. ''I bet you have some Civil War stories in yore history, Edna.''

''Some,'' Edna said. The others waited, silent except for the whisper of their hooks. ''A cousin six times or so removed on my mother's side was Champ Ferguson.''

''Really?'' Louella said, obviously thrilled. The others looked at both women blankly.

''He was a raider. Like Morgan. Only not so well-known because he got hisself caught and hanged,'' Edna said.

''The story was he was no raider, but a renegade,'' Louella said. ''Morgan ware regular Confederate under command of Braxton Bragg. He never made a raid unless ordered—well, except for the Ohio raid that got him captured, Morgan did that against orders. But Ferguson, he was wanted by both sides, Confederate and Union, for stealing and murdering. It was the Federals who tried him. Ferguson's defense was he was a regular soldier following orders, but he couldn't produce any enlistment documents. Besides, the Union had witnesses that he'd murdered captured soldiers and that'd be a crime whether he was army or not. So they hung him.''

''He was that violent?'' Bertha asked.

''Story was his wife and daughter had been humiliated by Union troops, and that made him mad. Another story was he was a murdering hill rowdy before the war and was just taking advantage of it.''

''None of that's true,'' Edna protested. ''He ware a patriot, he ware one of the first patriots.''

''What do you mean by that, honey?'' Louella spoke with an odd gentleness, Molly noticed; her voice had been sharper while telling the tale. What's going on here? Molly thought.

Edna looked intently at her piecework. ''What do you think, Louella, are my joiner stitches getting too tight, are they gonna pull at these squares?''

''No, dear, they look just fine. That word 'patriot,' usually they say 'Rebel,' even in Kentucky.''

''Oh, they called themselves that sometimes,'' Alyce Wheeler said then. ''Or freedom for—''

Edna interrupted her. ''I had another relative who's kinda interesting, too. He was a Yankee who when he heard Negroes were to be emancipated, resigned in protest. He wrote his letter of resignation sayin' he could in no way support the war now that it was for the Negro, adding that the service could not possibly suffer by his resignation. His commanding officer, in puttin' out a warrant for his arrest, noted on the document that it was true, the service could not possibly suffer without his services.''

The women laughed at that story, and soon were trying to top each other again. Mary O'Dell produced another ancestor, a captain of the Confederacy who, when wounded, had been tended by sympathizers behind Union lines. When healed, he tried to sneak back to the Confederate lines, but had been spotted by Union pickets. He tried to pass through by pretending to be a West Virginia farmhand looking for a steer. Trouble was, his boots were too expensive and his accent, much as he tried, just wasn't hillbilly enough to fool the pickets. So they got him.

Then Bertha took a turn telling about an aide to one of her ancestors who was really stupid. The officer handed the aide a pouch of tobacco for safekeeping and at the same time asked the man to make him some tea. The aide thought he wanted tea made from the tobacco. That story elicited ughs all around.

The stories droned on and before Molly was aware that the afternoon had passed, the veil was finished, and Zenith and Betty were at the door to take everyone home. Molly modeled the veil for the women, who oohed and aahed and declared they couldn't wait to see that pretty daughter of hers in it come next Saturday. And then they were gone.

Molly and Louella cleaned up together. ''You're very quiet, Louella,'' Molly said. ''What are you thinking?''

''I'm thinking we need to telephone the sheriff right away. This was a very productive session, the first one where we've got something to report.''

Molly stared at her; what was she babbling about?

Louella saw her expression and spluttered. ''I say, gal,

don't you know how to listen to women talk? Somethin' really happened today. Edna changed the subject.''

"Changed the subject?"

"Yes. Now maybe a man changes subject all the time, and it don't mean nothing, but women finish their stories. Edna changed the subject. Don't you see? She changed the subject. What's more, when Alyce tried to help out by finishing up for her, Edna interrupted. Don't you know what an interruption means?''

"????" Molly choked in confusion.

"Men interrupt all the time, that's jist how men are, but a woman'd never interrupt another woman 'less she's got reasons, big reasons. We gotta call John, now."

FOURTEEN

GIRL TALK

"Is it true..." Molly began.

"Hmm?" Ken said. He was in his study busily scanning the messages on Amanda's wedding Web site. There were scores because the wedding was now only two days away. Some reenactors were expected to arrive tomorrow, Friday, to set up their campsites, and these people had lots of last-minute questions. It was so early the sun was not quite up yet and the prelight of the dawn, although bright enough to read by, was soft, gentle. This would be Molly's favorite time of day—if it weren't so damned early.

Molly sat in a chair in Ken's spacious, tidy study. His desk, actually an old slab supported by file cabinets, was bare of stray papers, the opposite of her own desk at the Meal Van headquarters. She sat quietly—mainly because she was still very sleepy—sipped her coffee, and worked on her morning to-do list.

"Is it true that you talk about gender issues in one of your sociology courses?" she asked.

"Yeah, Sosh Two, Sociology 102, American Culture, I do about a week on gender. Why?"

"Is it true that women speak differently than men? I mean, women say so all the time; I can't think of a gathering of women where someone doesn't say that girl talk is special, but is it? Is there scientific proof for such differences?"

Ken turned to look at her, a puzzled frown on his face. "Good morning, Molly. Sure you don't want to talk about the weather, quantum physics, the nature of faith, something lighter and more accessible than gender differences?"

"I just want to know, is all."

She wondered why she could not tell him. It wasn't as if Louella had sworn her to secrecy. Louella had done no such thing. All she had done last week was tell John firmly that she was sure now that he should be watching the Farons and the Wheelers in this gun-smuggling thing.

"Which Farons?" Matins had asked.

"I'd say Dwight, the young boy, Edna Faron's grandson, but maybe her son, Samuel, too. Either way, a Faron's in it. And Robert Wheeler is a possibility, too. I'm not so sure there, but he'd be worth time to eye, too."

Matins, as in a hundred confrontations before with Louella, had narrowed his eyes, and asked, "How can you be so sure?"

"I'm jist sure."

"Louella, you tell me why."

She had glared at him for his impertinence.

"Please?"

Glare.

"Now, Louella, I can't even question someone unless I have cause."

"I din't say question, I jist said keep an eye on 'em until you do have cause. I done my part as you asked, I been listenin'. I listened. I say Farons and Wheelers."

"Well, yeah, Louella, but I kinda need to know what you heard."

She had straightened to her full four-foot-eleven-inch height, using her cane to push herself erect. "I'm no common gossip; I told you all I care to," she hissed.

He had looked at her a few seconds more and, as in those same hundred times before, backed down and gone to do exactly as she told him to. He went by to say howdy to Dwight and Samuel at the truck yard where they worked, and he stopped by Zenith's nursery to chat with Robert about, oh, nothing, and he found excuses to keep dropping by. It bothered Molly to think how thin were the reasons that had put a sheriff after those men.

"Sure would help to know what Louella knows," he said to Molly after a couple days of this. "Do you know, Molly?"

"No," she lied. Louella had been right too many times in the past for her to tell him how flimsy was the "evidence." As far as she knew, Louella's tips might always have been this flimsy. One change of subject by Edna Faron, one interrupted interjection from Alyce Wheeler. That was it. Their men were involved in something, Louella was sure, just because the girl-talk clues said so. Molly didn't dare tell John what she knew. He'd never believe anything either of them said again. "No, Louella never tells me anything, you know that, John."

He'd narrowed his eyes at her, too, mainly because he knew a lie when he heard one. "Molly, I'll tell you plain, sometimes you are just as native as a native."

"Is that a compliment, John?"

"It would be if I weren't so damned aggravated at you both. By the way, that veil you all made for Amanda is the prettiest thing I ever did see."

"Louella and her friends made it. I just brought the food."

"In other words, flattery will get me nowhere," he sighed.

"Did it ever, John?"

So she'd managed to deflect Matins's doubts, but not

her own. Was a slight tremor in a woman's conversation enough to detect criminal activity? She didn't have the confidence Louella had in these things. Which was why, after nearly a week of brooding about it, she finally asked her husband, in his role as Dr. K, about gender and speech.

"I just want to know," she repeated to Ken. "Have there been any scientific studies on gender differences in speech patterns?"

"Okay, let me finish here." He keyed in replies to a few more queries, posted the latest weather forecast for the wedding ("mild temperatures, sunny"), and typed a new item in the "Who's Coming" link ("NEW: Cincinnati high-school history teacher plans to be a 'British' observer with the Confederacy"). He checked a couple other links and shut down. "Looks like we have more Confederates coming than Union. Hope some of them will galvanize, or the Union will lose on Saturday."

Molly smiled. She hadn't given him his oilcloth coat yet. She planned that surprise for tomorrow morning, a wedding present for the father of the bride.

"Okay, gender," he said. "Odd that you're interested now. My wild-card course is coming up next semester and I was thinking of doing something like Women and World Cultures, so I've been collecting lots of stuff." The college let Ken do a course of his choosing every other semester. They required him to teach Beginning Sociology and American Culture, plus three advanced courses—Social Problems, Crime and Poverty, and Appalachian Culture. That left one course of his six-course allotment up to him. He liked to work up new courses for that slot, to keep from being bored, as he put it. Past wild-card courses had included Media and Society, Technology and Society, America and Its Minorities, The Sociology of Sport, Food and Society, and Art and Society. Amanda had talked him into the art course; Todd had suggested the food course. He wanted to do a gender course, he said, because, well, it was time. It was the hottest field in social science.

He had opened one of the file drawers. Molly loved it when he did that. Each drawer was a treasure chest which he readily shared whenever she asked. Amanda and Todd might joke about "the man who never talks when he can lecture," but she enjoyed him because he read so much. "This whole drawer is stuff on gender issues; I think I made a folder on interpersonal communication." He became absorbed in one of the folders.

Molly waited. Molly sipped. Molly added items to her list. Finally she said. "Ken?"

"Oh, sorry. Well, let's see, what do you want? The simple answer or the involved?"

"The simple."

"The simple answer is, some studies say there are profound differences in women's conversational styles, that there is a distinct women's culture within American culture. These studies tend to be written mostly by women. Other papers say such studies are inconclusive, that their methodologies are flawed, that the evidence for such differences is not compelling. These studies tend to be written by men." Ken smiled, shrugged.

That was another thing she loved about him. He was a sociologist who could admit that sociology was often very silly. "Is there anything specific in any of those inconclusive studies, anything that says *how* these women and men inconclusively differ?" she asked.

"This one, 'The Bases for Differing Evaluations of Male and Female Speech,' argues that sex-role stereotypes account for speech differences."

"Can you translate that?"

"Now, Molly, that was in plain English. You didn't understand?"

"My sex-role stereotype must be confusing me."

"It just means that any differences are learned behavior."

"Anyone with ten cents' worth of sense knows that," Molly groused. "I want to know *how* the sexes talk differently, not *why*."

"Okay, let's see, here's one that shows men open conversations depending on how sexy they think a woman is, but women don't care so much about that. A woman will talk to a homely man if she thinks he's interesting. Here's one that says conversational differences have nothing to do with sex, but a lot to do with similarity in levels of dysphoria."

"Ken, I bet even you don't know what 'dysphoria' means," Molly huffed.

"Oh, yes, I do. That's the kind of word you only have to look up once in a lifetime. You never forget it." He saw her scowl, and hastily added, "Right, sorry. It means anxiety or depression. This study says the more similar people are in levels of anxiety, the more likely they are to have a satisfying conversation."

"So the saying 'misery loves company' is statistically verified?"

"Chi squares and all. Okay, what else do I have in here?" He was shuffling through papers as if they were recipe cards. "Here are two that say hormones affect conversation. One showed that elderly women taking estrogen supplements were better at self-expression than women who didn't take supplements. This one says males high in testosterone are less able to express themselves verbally. This one says both male and female abused children are poorer at self-expression as adults. And this one says the high interruption rates of males are associated with low feelings of social inadequacy.''

Molly frowned, trying to puzzle the phrase through. ''Low inadequacy, double negative equals positive; I get it, the more of a bastard you are, the more likely you are to interrupt.''

Ken laughed. ''Exactly right. Okay, here's another one that says social roles, not gender roles are the real shapers of conversational skill, but here's one in the same issue of the same journal that says the opposite, that it's gender roles, not social roles. In other words, it argues that women and men have rigidly defined roles which in turn create separate cultures and separate cultures means separate language or conversational styles.''

''I see what you mean by inconclusive. What do you think?''

''I think common sense tells us there are differences in the way men and women speak and the kinds of things they talk about, but social science hasn't yet figured out how to measure or describe them. There are so many variables—topics, education of speakers, relationship of speakers, activity while talking—all could be as important or more important than gender. Plus the scientific jargon to describe conversation is in its infancy. For example, what words should we use to describe minute differences in conversational gambits? You just now asked me what I think. 'What do you think?' were your exact words. What if you had said, 'Can you tell me what you think?' or 'Would you tell me what you think?' or, 'Tell me what you think.' Each phrasing suggests a different kind of relationship. The 'tell me' form would be a command, you would be saying you're superior to me. The 'would you' form puts you beneath me, as weaker than me. The 'can you' is an attack; it questions my competence to answer. The way you actually phrased it suggests a dyad of equals. Dyads are pairs. These studies love that word 'dyad.' It's 'dyad' this and 'dyad' that all through them.''

"Sounds like a species of insect.''

"Linguistics, the study of grammar, has some terms for conversational strategies. There's the Proffer, the Counter, the Satisfy, the Reject, and the Accept. But there's so much more to a conversation than grammar. Terms to label who talks, who listens, when both are silent, when both talk at the same time, and abrupt subject changes haven't been invented yet, although a new discipline, sociolinguistics, is trying to. But until they do, how can we measure what we can't even name?''

"Tell me about those abrupt subject changes,'' Molly said, leaning forward intently. Ken didn't notice her change of body position.

"I don't have anything in this file. If it's been studied, I haven't found it yet, and I've been warping all the Web search engines about this. It's a frustrating topic. Too much opinion. Too little fact.''

"Do you have anything on same-sex conversations, women talking to women?''

He looked through the file again. "Nothing. Everybody wants to know about courtship, not friendship. No, wait, here's something, an old paper, 1972, it counted the minutes women spent talking together about different topics. They talked about clothes more than they did men.''

"That's not how women I know talk,'' Molly said indignantly.

Ken shrugged. "Studies are artificial setups. People are invited to an unfamiliar place, asked to sit with strangers, and then told to act naturally.''

"Wasn't there a recent best-seller on conversation?"

"Yeah, I'll use it if I do the course, Deborah Tannen's *You Just Don't Understand.* But I have another book here I like a lot, too expensive for my students to buy, but maybe I'll use it for reserve readings. It's *Grooming, Gossip and the Evolution of Language.* It's an anthropology text attacking the usual theory that early man evolved language as a hunting aid. Language really evolved to replace group grooming, this author argues instead. Grooming creates social cohesion in all groups of primates."

"Every ape has to scratch some other ape?"

"Yeah, but as human groups grew larger, taking time to groom everyone in the community in order to bond with them all took too much time, so language was substituted. A 'hello' was faster than a back rub."

"By that theory then, conversation must have been invented by women, not men," Molly said.

"Maybe women talk more than men today because they invented the whole thing to begin with."

"I like that theory. Did a woman write the book?"

"No, a man."

"I like that theory a lot."

"I thought you would."

"Would you like a back rub instead of a conversation?"

"I thought you'd never offer."

"So women invented conversation?"

"It's just a theory, Molly."

"A man would say that."

FIFTEEN

HOOPS

KEN, resplendent in his new oilcloth coat with its brilliant grapes, intense peonies, and meandering ivy, bowed deeply in the doorway of their bedroom. "Madam, you are beautiful," he said. "Will you journey with me to the site of tomorrow's wedding?"

Molly wailed, "I'm fat. I look awful."

"No, you look fine."

"No wonder they wore those corsets. My waist looks normal in jeans and a top, but in this, I look like a flopping walrus."

"Yes," Ken said, "you'd look better in a short, black-lace teddy, but, still, there's something to be said for Victorian dress. It's mysterious, sensuous. Trust me, you'll be the belle of the ball, excepting for the bride, of course."

Molly took a tentative step. Her navy blue skirt swayed like a buoy in rough waters. "I think I'm going to be seasick."

"I think you just need some practice. Come, m'lady, may I escort you around the veranda?"

"Are you being gallant or just insufferable?"

He smiled as if the answer were obvious.

"All right, all right," she complained. "I did promise to do this for Amanda's wedding. I'll be a good—no, correction, I'll be a silent martyr. Good is too much to ask of me."

Molly then proceeded to wail loudly at every obstacle on their way to the reenactment. How was she going to get in and out of the car; how was she going to sit on the seat; how was she going to stand two days without glasses; how could she walk in these impossible high-button shoes; how would she manage both days without a purse? Victorian ladies carried small pouches or baskets instead of purses. Molly had a basket, but her crochet and wireless phone filled it completely. There was no room for anything else except a coin purse and her driver's license.

After several miles of this noise, Ken said, "I thought you were going to be a *silent* martyr."

That quieted her. When they left the parking lot behind them and crossed the road into the campgrounds, they also crossed into the nineteenth century—the illusion was that strong. The trees, not yet fully leafed out, scattered the early-morning sunlight into dancing shafts which caught the thin, rising smoke from the campfires and turned it golden. Barely visible in this splendid haze were soldiers, Union soldiers, judging by the darkness of their jackets.

The soldiers stood in twos and threes, talking and drinking coffee from tin cups. Some sat on hay bales, polishing their leather or cleaning their guns. Some wrote letters. Some napped. A few were in shirtsleeves—muslin, calico or gingham off-the-shoulder, pullover shirts with underarm gussets typical of the period. They wore suspenders, not belts. Their pants were very loose and of a sky-blue, not dark blue, color. Their hats were of every shape and size imaginable; apparently the squat kepi was not required by Union regulations. The men looked exactly like antique photos she had seen of Union soldiers, except they moved, they breathed, and they filled the haze with their soft voices.

They touched caps at sight of her, but did not speak. She remembered Amanda telling her that nineteenth-century etiquette forbade men from addressing ladies unless the lady spoke first.

"Good morning, gentlemen," she said, trying to remember the polite Victorian phrasing Amanda had taught her. She was determined not to be a "mannequin," reenactor slang—and an insult—for a person who dresses the part but does not act it.

"Morning, ma'am, fine morning," one said.

"Gentlemen, a lady is present, put your jackets on," a sergeant snapped.

"A restful night?" Molly said to the group.

"No Confederate activity that we know of, ma'am."

"So no wounded for me to tend yet."

"Oh, are you the nurse? Then you be the mother of the bride." The man's expression changed from pretend to real. "How do you do. Gentlemen, this is Mrs. West, Amanda's mother."

Instantly she was surrounded by a crowd of eager Union infantrymen. "This is so nice of you to share your wedding with us like this.... Amanda said this is the first time you've been a reenactor.... May we show you around?...Would you like some coffee?" She was whisked away from Ken, although one of the men politely told him that the Confederate camp was "over there," adding that it might be too warm for a slicker today. He meant the oilcloth coat.

A scant glimpse of another campsite showed through the trees. Remnants of morning mists also shrouded these farther soldiers, as did the underbrush. But the Confederates were obviously much closer than they would have been in 1862, more like within a modern football's toss. Ken bowed to her and headed in that direction.

"Ken."

He turned.

"You don't have to wear that stupid coat, you know."

"Molly, if I'm killed in the battle tomorrow, I want to be buried in this coat."

"Come home to me in one piece," she called. He would stay in the Confederate camp tonight, and since she was a Union nurse, she'd be in this camp. It was considered bad form for a uniformed soldier to be in the other's camp before the battle, although they could visit the neutral civilian camp where the sutlers and the crafts demonstrators were set up. She watched him walk away with his misshapen shoes and droopy slouch hat. His canteen, cup, and blanket dangled from his pack—his "haversack," she now knew it was called. His rifle was awkwardly slung over his shoulder and that ridiculous floral coat flapped against his rump. He was a sight, but she felt for just a second as if he really were leaving, that there was a war out there.

"We're about to have the morning inspection of troops, Mrs. West. We'd be honored if you'd be our guest." The Union captain was speaking to her.

"Why thank you, Mr.—I mean—Captain. I regret I do not know your name." Was that appropriately florid enough for Victorian conversation? she wondered.

"I do apologize, ma'am. Captain Donegal, Ohio 92nd, at your service." He offered his arm, she took it and let him whirl her away into a dreamworld. He led her between two precisely aligned rows of white canvas. These were dog tents, not pup tents—that term was to come later, in World War I. Each was stretched taut over rope or branches and set so near the next one they looked tight as hens on a roost. An occasional glass lantern hung on a tent pole, although most poles were festooned with canteens, haversacks, and cartridge boxes instead.

Straw covered the ground inside each tent. A few blanket-covered straw pallets filled the rare spaces between the tents. These must have been where the hardcores slept, Molly thought, also called stitch counters or thread counters—reenactor slang for the opposite of mannequins, that is, people who took the game a little too seriously, and again an insult.

Ground fires, three of them, were placed at the row's center and served the cooking needs of the company. A private came forward with a camp stool and folding table for her. "How on earth do you find these reproductions?" she exclaimed.

"We get most of our gear from sutlers," the private explained, "but this stool and table came from Wal-Mart," he said with a shy grin.

She laughed. The troopers were moving briskly now, buttoning jackets, adjusting caps, and retrieving their rifles from the stockpile.

The inspection was serious business, Molly quickly saw. An experienced reenactor, not a member of this company, had been specifically invited by the quartermaster to serve for the entire event. Troops called him "the god." His job was safety first and accuracy second. He had to check all guns to be sure they would fire safely and to approve all gear for authenticity. "If the gear is too farb or the gun unsafe, the reenactor can be removed from the event," Captain Donegal explained.

"Farb?" Molly said.

"Inauthentic or too modern—anachronisms."

"What a wonderful word. Where does it come from?"

"No one knows, although the story is that it's after a

stitch counter who always began his criticisms of someone else's gear with the phrase, 'Far be it from me to criticize, but…'"

"A fine insult. I'm enjoying this reenactor slang," Molly said.

"Well then, what other words can I delight you with? People whose gear is too 'farb' are either 'cowboys' or 'fresh fish.' Fresh fish are guys new to reenacting. We call them that because their equipment shines and they stink, meaning they can't march very well. Or shoot either. Sometimes we call them 'hayfoots,' which was a real Civil War term for new recruits because some of them were so ignorant they'd never been taught left from right. Drill sergeants had to tie hay to their left feet and straw to the right—anyone in those days would know the difference—and call out 'hay foot, march' instead of 'left foot, march.'"

"So I'm 'fresh fish' then?" Molly said laughing.

"No, ma'am, you are an honored dignitary, and my guest. Although yonder, that woman who is clearly overdressed and will probably soon be overacting will be called a 'ham' or a 'Scarlett O'Hara.'" He meant a slight woman in a blond ringlet wig with tight corset and bright yellow dress with plunging neckline.

The soldiers had now lined up in front of their tents and held their rifles on the ground in front of them, pointing the muzzles slightly away from their faces as the inspector gently shoved a ramrod down each gun to be sure it was clean. "Dirty guns are dangerous," Captain Donegal explained. "Black powder is smoky, gummy. A plugged gun could put out an eye or tear off a finger. So the inspectors are pretty strict about guns, but will let farb gear by if they know the person is new to the hobby. Even so, every company carries a 'proof book,' a notebook with copies of photos or letters to show inspectors that our way of wearing insignia or type of gear was really the practice of the original company, in our case the Ohio 92nd.''

The inspector approached the captain, saluted, and reported his troops were fit for duty.

"Now if you will excuse me, ma'am," he said. He kissed her gloved hand. "Lieutenant, form the ranks," he said. Soon the soldiers were wheeling and turning and whipping their rifles on and off shoulders in the time-honored maneuvers prescribed in *Hardee's Tactics*, the 1861 drill manual by General William Joseph Hardee that was used by both sides. The soldiers moved rather awkwardly, she noticed, but, well, for many of them it was the first event of the season and they were out of practice.

She spent the rest of the day listening to stories, trading notes on costumes, and practicing and improving her own demonstrations. Few spectators were in camp today. Most would come tomorrow, Saturday. She had decided that in addition to showing Civil War-era first-aid techniques, she would also demonstrate crochet, perhaps give lessons. She hoped no one would notice her "farb" aluminum hook, though.

Several times that day she ran into Amanda in a plain calico dress, no hoops. "Tomorrow," Amanda said. "Today Dawn and I are too busy making sure everything is ready to fool with hoops. It's authentic enough. Poor women didn't wear hoops."

"I'm posing as her servant for the weekend," Dawn announced. "Her insolent servant," she hastily added when she saw Molly's raised eyebrow. "We oppressed peoples have ways of communicating our suffering.''

"I'm really impressed with the organization here,"

Molly complimented both of them. "You even have porta-toilets for the handicapped."

Amanda and Dawn had laughed. "It's not just the disabled who need those wider doors, Mom. A woman in a hoopskirt needs a big portal."

"Oh." She blushed to think about it. "How did women of the era stand the confinement of their clothes?"

"No, you're seeing it from our times," Dawn said. "To a Victorian lady the hoop was liberation. Before hoops, women endured fourteen, fifteen pounds of petticoats to spread their skirts. The Civil War was women's lib before lib was in. Not 'til the 1960s would women be as venturesome as they were then. The Civil War was the era of the woman social reformer. Women were working as laundresses, teachers, nurses, merchants, seamstresses, letter writers, cooks, and professional mourners. All these were careers newly open to women, mainly because of the shortage of men off at war. It was an exciting time to be a woman, and the hoop was symbol of all these changes."

"Congratulations, Mom, you've just heard your first haversack lecture," Amanda said.

"My what?"

"A short, impromptu talk when a reenactor shows off his or her knowledge, often *without being asked*." She hissed this last at Dawn.

Dawn shrugged. "Good lecture, though, right?" she bragged.

By day's end Molly was exhausted. She had admired Bently's fine lieutenant's uniform, which showed off his trim figure and blond hair better than any tuxedo would have. She had been allowed to pump the bellows for the blacksmith, wield a razor for the dentist/barber, try on the red jacket and black leather cap of the British observer, help curry the coat of a cavalry horse, mark a board with a carpenter's scriber, tap a new sole onto a soldier's brogan, and tend bar for a sutler. She had met over a hundred people, most from Ohio, but some from as far away as Pennsylvania and Maryland. The woman in the blond ringlet wig, the potential Scarlett O'Hara, turned out to be none other than Maria Jane Bently Cottingham Bellamy, Bently's mother, and the most provocative saloon girl ever. All she needed was a saloon.

That evening the troops sat around their separate campfires and competed with a sing-along of period tunes. First the South would offer a song, the Union would reply. Each side had a banjo player and a guitarist. The South had a fiddler and the sounds of it, muted by the bush between the camps, sent chills up Molly's spine. Molly wondered if it was Mary-Mary acting as a camp follower for the Rebels.

Later, in the hospital tent, she sat on her cot in a Victorian nightgown she had bought just for this event. As she took off her high-button shoes and stretched her aching feet, she thought that if tomorrow were half as much fun as today, this might be the first wedding in her life she actually enjoyed. She drifted off to sleep to the haunting wails of a solo harmonica. But aren't harmonicas farb? she wondered.

SIXTEEN

GIRL TALK

MORE REENACTORS and many spectators arrived Saturday morning, so by noon, when the troops were supposed to bivouac at their assigned spots, there were about five hundred people in the campgrounds. Amy Faron's father-in-law, Samuel Faron, had not shown up with the wagon and team, but Amy said he had promised to come, he would get there eventually. Other than that, everyone who was supposed to be there was there, including the chaplain who, until the ceremony, was posing as a raffish spy for the South.

Overnight, details had been worked out about who was to galvanize. Two horsemen who rode in splendidly braided and plumed Confederate gear on Friday were galloping through camp this morning in more sedate Union getup. One reined up sharply before the barber/dentist, who now was wearing the bright red shirt of the artillery. "I don't get to kill you today, after all. I'm on your side."

"Glad you're with the good guys for a change," the dentist gibed back.

By twos and threes, the Union men began slipping away into the woods. The plan was for Confederates to stay by the main campgrounds, in sight of the spectators' cordoned area, so that it would appear that the Rebels had been "surprised" by a Union scouting party.

Some spectators were in this ring already and had set

up lawn chairs for the best viewing. Why is it some people are never caught anywhere without a lawn chair or an umbrella? Molly wondered. Ken's answer to that query would be those of us without either are not meant to know such things. She wondered how he was doing. She'd caught a glimpse of him this morning when the Confederates were drilling. She'd been amused to see that the captain who was trying to whip them into shape was none other than Captain Donegal, who was now wearing a Confederate kersey jacket, that is, the gray, cotton/wool blend used by the South during wool shortages.

Kevin Logan, the quartermaster for the Ohio 92nd, a tall, rangy man whose uniform fit so poorly it defied even the baggy standards of the era, walked among the costumed women. "Ladies, declare your loyalties. We are assembling for battle," he said. He meant each woman should choose which line she would follow.

Union women were few this morning, perhaps because the best viewing was from the Confederate side. Whatever the reason, only eight women followed the Union escort, a private from Portsmouth, Ohio, named Jason Sherman, a distant relative of the great or the hated—depending on your point of view—William Tecumseh Sherman.

"With a name like that, how come you're a private, not a general?" Molly teased.

"We have to earn our rank, ma'am, same as in a real company," he replied.

The eight women walked quietly, except for the swishing of their skirts, to the rendezvous. In addition to Molly, the Union loyalists that morning were Louella; Amanda; Bently's mother, Maria Jane; Dawn Cannon; Connie Tanton; Lorraine DeWitt; and Sherry Matins.

Louella wore a sunbonnet and a poor woman's simple calico dress. A homestead dress, Amanda called it. The sunbonnet was her grandmother's, Louella said. She apologized for making the group slow down to an old woman's pace, but she and her family were Union forever; she couldn't be Rebel even for just pretend. All the other women, Dawn included, wore hoopskirts in strong if not bright colors—blues, greens, russets, maroons. Maria Jane had covered her yellow saloon girl dress with a brown cape because, someone had gently explained to her yesterday, not even a saloon girl went out in broad daylight with an exposed bosom.

They reached the Union formation well past the cabin, in deep woods. Molly, looking at the weed seeds sticking to her hem, understood why there were so many sudden Southern sympathizers this morning. The women didn't want to damage their expensive clothes. They found Captain Donegal and Bently in deep discussion, almost an argument, but both men broke into smiles at sight of the women. Bently kissed Amanda, then hugged his mother, lifting her off the ground.

"Mother, you are positively scandalous in that wig," he laughed. "Are you having fun?"

"I thought I'd hate every minute of this, but people are so nice. I've learned so much. You look so handsome in that uniform."

He smiled, and the women and the officers spent a minute or two exchanging introductions.

"I see you've rejoined the Union cause," Molly teased Donegal.

"I never left it, ma'am; that man you saw in Rebel kersey, he was just helping their Awkward Squad drill. He wasn't really me."

"If it's not too impertinent of me to ask," Amanda began, "what were you and the captain discussing so intently when we interrupted you?" Molly could not believe this polite lady was her sassy Amanda. Too bad Victorian etiquette didn't rub off into everyday life.

"We are still a little short of Union troops," Captain Donegal said, "and as it is Lieutenant Cottingham's wedding day, we've decided as a wedding present to give him a chance to be the hero."

"I really don't think they should do this," Bently said.

"Hush, Bently," said Maria Jane, "you obviously have no sense at all." Molly smiled. This must be the Maria Jane that Amanda feared.

"I propose to move the main troop north, away from the river, leaving a small force with you here. Our force will come in above the cabin," Donegal explained. "Then when we're fully engaged, the lieutenant's force will come in with a surprise flanking maneuver from west of the cabin. That will force them to split their forces and let us carry the day."

"How will we communicate?" Bently said.

"We have two cavalry officers. I'll send one back to tell you when it's time to start moving forward."

Bently nodded his assent. The sergeants bawled orders, and soon two files of soldiers were moving north. When they were gone, only eleven men were left with the women.

Molly sat down on a stump. There was an hour to go before the start of the battle, and she planned to use the time to go over last-minute details of the wedding ceremony with Amanda.

While they were conferring, a man in Confederate garb—butternut jacket, flat-brimmed hat, faded blue pants, rough boots—stepped into the Union area. Bently smiled. "Confederate area's about a half mile that way, the other side of the cabin," he said.

"I ain't lost, buster," the man said. "You are."

"Now we agreed, it's our turn to surprise you. Besides, all action is to be where spectators can see."

"Spectators?" the man said, suddenly confused.

It was then almost everyone in the group noticed that the man's gun was no musket. Unlike the three-banded reproduction Enfields or Springfields the reenactors carried, his gun was a semiautomatic Rambo-style something or other. An M1? An AK-47? An Uzi? Molly wondered, although she wouldn't know an Uzi from a fuzzy-wuzzy, come to think of it.

"Um, that's not authentic Rebel arms," Private Sherman said.

"Are you with the reenactment?" Bently added.

"I don't know whut yer talkin' about and you don't belong here, this here's private."

"This is the Wayne National Forest," Bently said.

"Government cain't own property. It's our'n. Now you git."

Another three men, again with the flat-brimmed hats, butternut shirts, and jeans, stepped from the brush. They, too, had the Rambo guns.

"I think it's only coincidence they look like Confederates," Molly said. "I think those guns are for real."

"What's happening? Who's the picket on duty?" said the tallest of the new men.

"I am, sir," said the first man. "We've got some strang ers wh—"

"My god, it's the ATF," said the officer. He raised his gun. "All of you, drop your guns."

"Now see here," Bently said.

The officer fired a round over their heads. "Drop them." They dropped them.

"What is the matter with you people?" Amanda yelled. "Don't you know Civil War soldiers when you see them?"

"Soldiers? Quick, men, this is the attack we've been expecting. Okay, you know what to do. First, take these scouts—"

"What about the women, sir?" the picket said.

The officer of what Molly was now sure was a paramilitary group was trying to think and at the same time working hard to suppress a personal panic. It was as if he had spent years preparing for this and now that it was here he was terrified. The one thing he feared. How many years had he spent both hoping it would and hoping it wouldn't happen? The Feds had come to get them. How many were there? Well, first secure these scouts they'd surprised. Funny getups those, but they were Feds all right. For sure. Molly could almost read his thoughts as they flickered across his bewildered face. He was absolutely certain they were ATF or FBI—the hated government. It all would be funny except for one tiny detail, those guns.

"The women?" he said finally. Had the government stooped so low that they were using women as cover?

"Here, sir, I count eight of them."

"Right, well then. There's an abandoned cabin about a quarter mile east of here. We'll put them there."

"But that's my weddin—" Amanda began.

Sherry shook her head at her, silencing her.

One of the militia men motioned to the women to begin marching.

"You stay with them, corporal, and guard them. Someone will relieve you shortly.'' The corporal saluted and took up a position behind the women.

They walked slowly. They couldn't go any faster than Louella and her cane. The hoopskirts made for awkward walking, too. Behind them they could hear Bently trying once more to persuade the officer that they'd figured wrong, that this was just a group of Civil War hobbyists, not federal officers, and that—a thud and then silence. Amanda winced and started to cry silently.

At the cabin, the corporal made the women put their baskets by the door and ordered them to sit on the dirt floor opposite the door. He sat facing them, gun on his knees, leaning on the doorframe. All was silent except for the wing flutter of an occasional bird.

After a time they heard footsteps and the rustle of a hoopskirt. Bonnie stepped into the cabin with an armful of lilacs. The corporal took her flowers, tossed them out the door, and made her join the others. Bonnie had gasped when she first saw him, but then she, too, was silent.

Molly couldn't help staring at Bonnie's costume. Was this the same jeans-and-a-top Bonnie? Her dress was magnificent, a deep forest green with a slight texture to the fabric. The skirt was trimmed with a matching welt and ruffle below the welt. The bodice was trimmed with a row of mother-of-pearl beads, from waist to slightly off the shoulder, then narrow flanges flowed beside the beads, off the shoulder to cap the simple gored sleeves. The folds effectively deemphasized her problem bust, Molly noticed. The space between the beads was filled with intricate crewel embroidery in the same forest green as the fabric. It was the finest dress at the event.

Molly turned from the dress and began furiously thinking, trying to figure a way to get to the phone in her basket. She caught a movement out of the corner of her eye and turned to look. Louella was making imaginary crochet stitches in the air. Molly frowned in puzzlement; what did she mean? Louella would make a stitch, tilt her head toward the guard, stitch again, tilt. Suddenly Molly smiled. She got it.

"What is your name?" Molly said to the guard.

He shook his head.

"Right. No names. Okay, I will just call you 'George' then. George, this is very important. My daughter is getting married very soon, and I'm crocheting her a wedding veil. I need to be working on it all the time or I won't have it finished in time. You do understand, don't you? Do you have children?"

Amanda gaped at her mother. Had she completely lost her mind? Amanda knew perfectly well that her veil was done and ready for the ceremony. She'd modeled it for everyone last night. It had been the talk of the camp— an authentic Victorian veil, one even the stitch counters couldn't find fault with. What was her mother thinking?

"Well, you know how important it is, to keep your word," Molly went on. "I promised my girl a veil and, well, my crochet is in my basket over there. There's a phone in there, too. I know you don't want me to have that, but if I could just have the ball of twine and my hook. I have so little time until her wedding to get it done."

By now all the women were staring at her as if she were nuts—except for Louella, who was smiling slightly. George, however, was frowning. "My wife, she likes to crochet, too," he said.

"May I then? It's so important to my daughter."

"Well, what harm can it do," he said. "Which basket is your'n?"

"The one with the dark red cloth on top."

He took out the twine, hook, and half-worked square and handed them to her. She began slowly to work her stitches. After a few seconds of silent work, she picked up a small broken twig and scratched a Y in the dirt floor. "What shall we talk about, girls?" she said. All at once all the women, except for Maria Jane, smiled. The chromosomal imperative. Of course.

"I'm having such trouble with my hair lately," Amanda said. "Maria Jane, yours is so beautiful. How do you keep it like that?"

Maria Jane, still puzzled, said nothing.

"What about you, Connie? Yours is looking nice today."

"I had it done this morning. You know that new hairdresser at the department store is almost good. But none of us are as cute as you are, Dawn. Who does your hair?"

"No one does black hair in this area. I go to Cincinnati. I have to go on buying trips for the factory and the store anyway, so I get my hair done then."

"Really? I never knew that," Bonnie said. "I never thought. But of course, in a region with few blacks, what would you do for a beauty shop? I want you to know, I've special ordered some black cosmetics for the store."

"Well, thank you. You are so sweet," Dawn said, and she meant it.

The women fell into silence again. Molly wiggled her hand in the chatter sign. Bonnie nodded, accepting the challenge. "I've ordered some products for dry skin, too, Lorraine. You said your skin was getting dry patches."

"That it is, especially around my eyes and nose. What do you do for crow's-feet? Is there any special treatment?"

"I've got two creams that should help."

"I just put a little olive oil on mine," Connie said.

"Doesn't the smell bother you?"

"I mix it with rosewater."

Louella was studying George's face. She shook her head. At that moment Maria Jane caught on to the game. "I'll tell you the secret of my hair, girls," she said. "Wigs. They're making them so natural these days, and the best part is you can leave your hair at the hairdresser's while you go shopping." George yawned.

Louella smiled, then nodded toward Amanda. "More," she mouthed. Amanda frowned, searching her imagination for a topic.

"I've been looking for a new catalog company for office wear. I'm very tired of the sporty look."

"Me too. Skirts and sweaters, knit dresses, that's all any of them show. I'd like a good old-fashioned shirt-waist."

"What about those houndstooth suits some of the catalogs are showing?"

"I like those, and the glen plaids, too."

George scratched, yawned again.

Amanda tried weight next. "Lorraine, you are getting so skinny. Are you on a diet?"

"No, but I am eating less meat these days."

Louella frowned and Amanda nodded. "Sherry, still having problems with your period?" The women's eyes opened wide at that topic, but, well, a desperate situation demanded a desperate strategy.

"All the time. I'm still having those awful cramps. Talked to the doctor, and he said having a baby is all I need."

"That's true," Maria Jane said. "I used to have the worst periods, then after Bently, I was as regular as clockwork. No cramps at all."

"I had cramps until I was twenty-two. Birth-control pills helped me. Cleared up my skin, too," said Connie.

George was now definitely fidgeting.

With a nod, Louella signaled Amanda to up the conversational stakes once again. "Well, I've been having trouble with a real heavy flow, really bloody. Should I worry?" Amanda said.

"That can be caused by fibroids," Lorraine said.

"Fibroids? I know a woman who had those. She had to have a hysterectomy. They can be serious," Sherry said.

"I thought it was just another side effect of the pill," Amanda said.

"How heavy is the flow?" Maria Jane asked.

"Well, I have these large clots that—"

George stood up abruptly, obviously agitated, then seemed to remember he couldn't leave the cabin, so he pretended to stretch instead and sat back down, gun once again over his knees.

"Clots?" Maria Jane gasped, forgetting, apparently, that the goal of the conversation was to remove George. She sounded actually concerned for Amanda.

"Yes, I'm worried. Is this normal or should I see a doctor?" Amanda said.

"I'd see a doctor," Molly said.

"Doctors only tell you to get pregnant," said Connie.

"Well, it is a solution," Maria Jane said.

Louella grimaced and Amanda took that as a cue to up the stakes one more time.

"Was Bently an easy birth, Maria Jane?"

"No, he was big, almost nine pounds. I was in labor forever. I had so many tears, I lost count of the stitches they put in me."

George shuddered.

"I didn't have a doctor, just a midwife," Louella said. "Both my babies tore me up real awful. The midwife had to sew me up, but we had no anesthetic. She just took a needle and stitched. I about died from screaming."

It wasn't just George who was shuddering at that.

"Well, I had a caesarian," Dawn said.

"I didn't know you'd had a child," Amanda said.

"It was stillborn. I had to have a caesarian to deliver the fetus, a horrible experience to be going through and knowing I'd already lost the baby. And there's just as much blood after a caesarian as after a normal birth, let me tell you. I passed bloody discharge for days and days and days after—"

George was on his feet again. This time he pretended to fumble for a cigarette. "I'll just take a smoke outside," he said.

Molly instantly switched from her soft double crochets to huge looping stitches, trying to turn the delicate twine into rope.

"Lord, I thought he'd never leave," Amanda whispered. "I was beginning to run out of topics."

"I waren't worried," Louella said. "We still had menopause to go. And we coulda done more wi' that hysterectomy thing, too."

"Keep talking," Sherry said. "Don't give him a reason to come back in."

"Boy, Dawn, to lose a baby like that. How awful for you," Bonnie said with real sympathy.

"I made that up," Dawn said.

"Wow," Connie said. "You are *good*."

"I figured if he were squirming at Louella's midwife

story, a nasty caesarian would push him over the edge. And it did.''

"So you've never been pregnant?" Amanda said.

"No."

"Does somebody bleed just as much after a caesarian?" Bonnie asked.

"How the hell would I know?" Dawn said.

"What about you, Louella? Was that a real story or made up?" Molly said.

"It ware real."

The conversation now settled into more normal topics, clothing and jobs and men. If the chatter lagged, Louella asked a question or told a story of her own, but she never took her eyes off Molly's flying hands. Molly hooked the twine as fast as she could, but still the rope was too short. Then she noticed that the stick she had used to draw the Y had a nub on one end. She took it and began hooking the rope with it. Soon she had a length of tough, if ugly, lace, about eight feet long.

"Make an uproar when we're in position," she whispered to Amanda. She nodded to Sherry and the two began crawling toward the door. The two women crouched on either side of the door, the bizarre, intricate rope between them. Sherry nodded to Amanda.

"Oh God, a snake, a snake. It's a copperhead. Oh no, oh God," she screamed. Her screams were so convincing that Maria Jane was actually frightened, lifting her skirts trying to find it. The others just joined in the yelling, eeking and shrieking with grand gusto and flapping their skirts with mock terror.

George ran in, gun in hand. Sherry and Molly jerked the rope taut just as he crossed the threshold. He fell, hard. His gun hand flew up toward Sherry. She twisted the gun away from him and stood over him.

"Thanks for saving us from that snake," she said.

Molly took scissors from her basket and cut the crochet line in half. Amanda tied George's hands and feet. Sherry checked the security of the knots.

"I think that will hold him," she said. "All right. Lorraine, get Molly's phone and call 911." Molly shook her head. Of course, Sherry would put the phone phobic on the phone assignment, but Lorraine didn't hesitate. She dived for the basket and had dialed before Sherry had given another order.

"Bonnie, you take Louella back to the campgrounds. The rest of you go with her."

"There's no answer at the 911," Lorraine wailed.

"Damn," Sherry said. "Martha's probably out weeding her flowers instead of tending that phone. Take the phone with you and keep trying. Start walking toward the campgrounds, all of you. When you get there, tell them not to start the reenactment, to keep soldiers and spectators away from the cabin until we know what's going on. Can anybody here ride a horse?"

"I can," Connie said.

"Okay, get to the other Union site and tell them what's happened. Tell them to stay put until we know what we're up against. See if they'll lend you a horse so you can ride down to where the state police are parked. Tell them I saw four, but I don't know how many there are or what they're up to, but that they're armed with imports."

"Imports?" Molly said.

"Those aren't U.S. guns. I've never seen anything like them before."

Louella spoke up then. "When you find Matins, be sure to tell him that that so-called officer was Samuel Faron."

"You knew one of them?" Sherry said. "How come you didn't say so?"

"Didn't seem prudent to say 'howdy' at the time."

"I guess you're right," Sherry said with a grin. "Okay, everybody get back to the campgrounds. Be sure to keep people out of here."

"Where are you going?" Amanda said.

"To rescue our boys in blue."

"No, you're not, not by yourself you're not," Amanda said.

"Don't be silly, you're a civilian."

"I'm a trained Union soldier. Besides, that's my Bently out there."

"I'm coming, too. That's my son," Maria Jane said.

"You're all crazy," Molly protested. "Wait for the police."

"No," Sherry said. "If we wait, they'll bring in the ATF, a commando unit, helicopters, the press. We'll have a three-ring circus, a standoff, a shoot-out. People will get killed. If we do it ourselves, we'll just have a nice normal stalking and arrest. If we can keep the Feds out of here, things will die down, get quiet. If the Feds come in, every male in the Tricounty will join some militia." While she spoke, Sherry had retrieved her pistol from her basket and now stood gracefully in her maroon hoopskirt and matching peplum. Her black bonnet, tied primly beneath her chin, warred with the tough frown she wore as she checked the mechanism on her .38.

"You sound like my husband," Molly said. But you look wonderful, she thought. "Well, if it's my daughter that's going to stupidly run off into the woods to rescue your son, I guess I'm coming, too," she said to Maria Jane.

"I think not," Sherry said, and then she looked at the

faces of the wide-skirted ladies in front of her. "Right, I must have temporarily lost my wits to think you'd be sensible and get out of here. Okay, do any of you know how to handle this?" she said, lifting George's gun.

"I do," Amanda said.

Molly's jaw dropped open. Her little girl a gun nut?

Amanda shrugged sheepishly. "Bently and I took a survival course. It was fun. We can rappel, skydive, make a raft from logs, kayak in white water, skin a deer, do a little judo, and shoot just about any gun they make," she told her mother.

My little girl is a gun nut, Molly thought.

"Okay, bride, you're borrowing George's gun. Let's go," Sherry said.

"Bye, George. Nice talking to you," Dawn said.

Amanda rubbed the muzzle of the gun in her hands. "Talk about your 'something borrowed,'" she said. "No bride should be without one of these."

"As for your something blue, I have an idea where he might be," said Dawn.

PART FOUR

SOMETHING BLUE

SEVENTEEN

HOOPS

DAWN'S IDEA was they might have put the eleven Union soldiers down the sinkhole entrance to the caves behind the Barton Mansion. She was the only one who knew the way, so she led the five women to it through increasingly rougher woods. Amanda, who had often been under the opening, had never been over it, so she didn't know how to find it.

"It's easier to find when the leaves are off the trees in February," Dawn said, "but I think the landmarks will work now, too. You keep the mansion to your left until you see both the east chimney and the tip of Zachariah Point. Then you turn toward the mansion."

"How did you figure that out?" Molly said.

"That bit of knowledge has been part of my family for almost a hundred and fifty years," Dawn said.

A slight gap in the briars ahead marked the sinkhole. The five women crouched in a tangle of wild honeysuckle and autumn olive. The roof of the mansion was just visible above the oaks beyond.

"I wonder if Delta Force ever had to make a rescue in hoopskirts," Sherry complained in a whisper.

"We could take them off and attack in our bloomers," Molly suggested, also whispering. Dawn almost giggled, but Sherry silenced her with a frown.

"I'm afraid white bloomers will be too visible in this brush. I thought of that while we walking over and decided we were safer in these darker dresses. Also the skirts make bigger targets; harder to hit something vital."

Molly shivered, realizing for the first time how dangerous what they were doing might be.

"My bloomers are black," Maria Jane said. No one knew what to do with this fact, so they all were silent.

"Something's happening," Dawn hissed.

"Down," Sherry commanded.

All five women flattened against the ground unaware that, as they did so, all five hoops bounced up in the opposite direction. The hoops scalloped behind the brush, a series of colorful half shells with pairs of bloomers extending behind, four white, one black and lacy.

They watched as two men in the neo-Confederacy garb they'd seen before climbed out of the hole. The men looked into the deep woods as if trying to see something, and so faced away from the rainbow of hoops.

"What's over that way?" Sherry whispered.

Dawn said, "Not much. Mostly woods—almost to the Cincinnati suburbs."

"Any roads?" Molly asked.

"Just logging roads, I think."

"What could they be looking for?" Amanda said.

"Guns," Molly said. "My guess is they're waiting for a smuggling shipment to arrive."

Now it was Amanda's jaw that flopped open, but Sherry didn't seem surprised by the idea.

"Boy, they sure can pick days," Maria Jane said. "Hundreds of people in the woods. You'd think they'd be smarter than that."

"They had to know about it if Sam Faron was involved; I mean, he was supposed to be bringing that wagon and team. He, of all people, had to know there was a public event in the forest today," Amanda said.

"Yeah, why today?" Molly said.

"They knew about it, for sure. Look," Amanda said. Flo Wheeler just then climbed out of the hole and like the two men stood with her back to the hidden rescuers scanning the woods for something. She was dressed in a khaki pantsuit of poplin or twill—Molly couldn't tell from this distance. The loose-fitting jacket with stylish patch pockets was open to reveal a black-nylon shell and russet-and-green designer scarf.

"Flo is in this?" Sherry said.

"Louella said there was a Wheeler involved," Molly said. "Maybe Flo is the Wheeler, instead of Robert."

"Or in addition to," Sherry said.

"I gather Matins told you what's going on?" Molly said to Sherry.

"Yeah, and he's told you, too?"

"Yes."

"Dad was always a good one for Appalachian secrets," Sherry said with an affectionate smile.

"What's an Appalachian secret?" Maria Jane asked.

"Tell everybody and then swear them to secrecy."

"Will somebody tell *me* what's going on?" Amanda said.

"Matins thinks there's a gun-smuggling ring in the Tricounty, and Louella thinks Wheelers and Farons are involved. Looks like Flo's the Wheeler," Molly said.

"Louella?" Amanda said.

"She's Dad's chief of intelligence," Sherry said.

"Oh."

"I think Flo would have to be in on it," Dawn said. "How else would those guys know how to find this sinkhole?"

"Yeah, but your church can find it."

"Those good ol' boy types don't belong to my church."

"But with several hundred people roaming the woods today, why didn't they change dates for delivery?" Sherry said.

"Maybe they couldn't. Maybe they have to take shipments as they come, like it or not," Dawn said.

"Or maybe they're working on the opposite theory. Lots of people would be good cover. Maybe they're dressed like Confederates on purpose," Molly said.

"So how come that picket didn't know we were Union reenactors when he caught us?" Amanda said.

"Maybe they don't tell the rank and file everything. Maybe they're just using the militia guys to hide their smuggling ring."

"Interesting theory," Sherry said.

"It's not my theory. It's Ken's."

"If something's coming, we've got to act fast, before it gets here, so we can be the ones to receive those goods," Sherry said.

"What about the guys?" Amanda said.

"And rescue the guys, too. I meant rescue the guys first."

"I've got an idea," Molly said. "Amanda, where's your Confederate uniform? You brought it with you, didn't you?"

"Sure, just in case someone needed to galvanize."

"Where is it?"

"Up at the mansion. My Union blues are there, too, and my wedding dress."

"Where's Bently's Confederate uniform?"

"It's up there, too."

"Think his clothes will fit me?"

Amanda smiled. "You ought to be a spy. Let's go.

Sherry, that means you guys will only have that pistol while we're gone.''

"We won't do anything too stupid until we see you," Sherry said.

BOTH WOMEN were thoroughly scratched from blackberry and greenbriar canes by the time they broke through the woods into the mown area behind the mansion's kitchen. To make it easier to push through the brush, they'd stripped off their skirts once they were out of sight of the sinkhole and were carrying them.

The kitchen door was locked, but Amanda just flipped up the sash on one of the floor-to-ceiling windows and stepped in, barely stooping as she did so.

"Well, glad we don't have to climb a drainpipe or anything, I'm afraid of heights," Molly said.

"Uh-oh, Mom, if your plan goes wrong, you may have to suffer some heights. The only escape route out of those caves if we can't get back out through the house is over that awful ledge on the cliff face.''

"This will work.''

Amanda snatched some rope from a drawer in one of the Hoosier cabinets. Then the women rushed through the kitchen, past piles of dishes and boxes of food waiting to be set out for the buffet later. They both changed into Confederate clothes and went down into the tunnels through the basement.

Slowly they crept toward the sinkhole. Peering around a bend they saw only two militiamen. "We're in luck," Amanda whispered. With Flo and two militiamen at the surface, only two men were left below, and they had their backs to the tunnel and the women. Molly and Amanda could see the Union soldiers sitting in a circle beneath the hole. Amanda stepped to the center of the main tunnel, her finger to her lips. Bently saw her. She motioned him to come toward her and then, touching Molly's elbow, pulled her into a side cave to hide.

"I gotta pee," Bently said.

"Tough," one of the guards said.

"I gotta do more than pee," Bently said.

"Oh, hell. All right. Private, take him to one of the side caves and let him crap back there."

The guard rose. "Keep your hands up," he said to Bently and fell in behind him. When the guard passed Amanda, she stepped forward, put her gun to his armpit and her hand over his mouth. Bently turned and easily lifted the gun out of the startled guard's hands.

"Smooth," Molly said, impressed. "Couldn't have been slicker if you'd rehearsed it."

"Actually we did. Several times. In that course I told you about."

They tied the guard and put him in Bonnie and Amanda's room. "I need to borrow this," Molly said to him, and took his bandanna. Then Bently put his hands up and Amanda pretended to return him to the circle, where they repeated the poke-and-disarm maneuver again. This guard they tied up and put in the room Molly would forever think of as David Wheeler's room. Bently took the guard's shirt and hat first and put them on.

"You two aren't alone?" Bently said as they finished securing the guard.

"No, Sherry, Dawn, and your mother are here with us," Amanda said.

"Mom? I don't believe it. No cops?" he said.

"Sherry's a cop."

"Jesus H. Christ, you guys are nuts. These guys are for real."

"Do you know what they are waiting for?" Molly said.

"Guns, I think. But there's guns down here already, in several of the side caves, I heard them say."

"Could be they're waiting for someone to pick them up, or maybe there's more to be dropped off," Molly said.

"Let's find them," Amanda said.

"Look for ammo, too," Molly said.

"What are these?" Bently exclaimed when they opened a box. "Look." He pointed to some odd lettering on the stocks.

"Those aren't Chinese characters, are they?" Amanda said.

"No," said Bently.

"Cyrillic?" Molly said.

"Russian guns? They're smuggling Russian guns?"

"Are they dealing with the Russian Mafia?" Molly asked.

"Where's the ladder?" Amanda said.

"The others pulled it up to the surface."

"Well, it would be too dangerous to climb up toward armed people anyway," Molly said. "Okay, here's my idea. Arm everybody, and Amanda, you lead them through the house back to Sherry. Take some extra guns."

"What will you and Bently do?"

"We'll pose here as those two militiamen, so they don't get suspicious and think their captives are gone. Don't do anything until whatever is coming actually arrives. Sherry knows that, but make sure these guys know it, too."

Bently took the men well out of hearing range of the sinkhole and briefed them, telling them that anyone who wanted out of the mission should say so now. These were real guns, and those were real criminals out there. They were under no obligation to help out, but if they would etc., etc. All ten volunteered, which surprised Molly. One, it was dangerous and, two, some of the men had to be sympathetic with the militarists. Then she watched them handle the guns and realized that, like Amanda, they were thrilled by them. No one cared about the politics, they just wanted the adventure—and a chance to get even with the rascals who had kidnapped them.

Amanda led the soldiers back toward the mansion. Molly and Bently took up positions just below the sinkhole. Flo stuck her head in the hole. "Get ready," she said, then added, "Where are the prisoners?"

"Stuck 'em yonder in one of the side caves so they can't yell out an alarm," Bently said with a passable Appalachian accent.

"Good idea," Flo said.

"Could she be in charge?" Bently whispered to Molly. "She sure sounds bossy."

"Where'd a nice Cleveland boy like you pick up a hillbilly accent?"

"I've served the Southern cause at quite a few reenactments now."

Flo's head was back over the sinkhole. "They're here. Both of you get up here and help unload the wagon." She and one of the others lowered the ladder back down. Bently climbed it, Molly following. She had pulled her slouch hat low over her forehead and hoped that the hat and the borrowed bandanna would keep Flo from recognizing her.

"Hey, Molly," Bently said, leaning down to whisper to her, "that scarf is farb."

"It is?"

"Yeah; bandannas of that era were checkered or solid. The railroad paisleys came later."

"Well, sorry. Next time I'll get it right."

He laughed.

EIGHTEEN

SCARF

THEY STEPPED FREE of the hole and briars, but kept their heads down, using their hat brims to shadow their faces. Flo wasn't looking at them anyway. She was still gazing intently toward the west and toward what was now a definite crashing nearby.

"Sam, honey, is that him, or is that some of those idiot reenactors?"

"Can't tell, babe. Sounds heavy. A wagon would sound like that."

Honey? Babe? Molly thought. She watched the two for a minute and decided that Sam and Flo were definitely an item. Could that be the reason Bonnie and Amy were tense with each other? Could it have made them uneasy to know that the breakup of Sam's marriage might have been Flo's doing? Sam looked like every local she'd ever met—thin, thin hair, weather-seamed skin, not handsome, not homely. She noticed his hands as they tightened on the gun as the sounds got closer. They were a mechanic's hands, at once callused but delicate, able to tenderly position a thin ignition wire or twist a stiff gasket. They were good hands for a gun, she thought as she tightened her own grip on her gun. She hadn't the foggiest idea how to fire it and hoped that gesturing with it would be enough.

The rustle and snapping intensified. Odd there were no engine sounds, she thought, and then she saw why. Two huge draft horses, grayish black with pale manes and tails, broke into sight, pulling Sam's bright green-and-gold wagon. Over the years she had often seen that wagon at county fairs or in parades, but she'd never known whose it was before. The drover was a younger edition of Sam, right down to the hands. Dwight, she guessed, and that was confirmed when she heard Flo snap at him by name and complain of his lateness.

"That logging road isn't much of a road," Dwight defended himself. "Probably hasn't been used since the last time we came through."

Bently touched Molly's elbow and pulled her back away from the wagon and into a crouch just as Flo and Sam and the other guard moved toward it. None of the others noticed. Sam and Flo put their guns down on the wagon seat and pulled open the tarp covering the cargo.

"Where's the courier?" Flo said.

Dwight laughed. "He's allergic to horses. Had to get off and walk. He'll be along shortly."

They all laughed then, but stopped in mid-laugh. Dwight's eyes opened wide as Sherry stood up. She had shed her hoopskirt but still wore her black bonnet and maroon bodice. Her stance, even though more often seen on women who wear leather, was no less intimidating on a woman in muslin drawers. Flo and Sam both reached for their guns. "I wouldn't do that if I were you. Hands up, all of you," Sherry said.

"Corporal," Flo yelled to the still-armed guard, "get her." He swung toward Sherry, but at that moment Bently jumped up and fired over his head. The guard froze. Dawn, still in her cadet blue hoopskirt and bodice with matching bonnet, now stood up with her gun. Then two of the Union soldiers with theirs, then Sheriff Matins in John Deere cap and plaid shirt, then several more soldiers, then Amanda in her Confederate hat and jacket and then lastly Maria Jane—all rose one at a time and pointed their borrowed guns at the smugglers.

The sunlight, still fragmented by the half-fledged trees, bounced off their guns. They stood, easily the strangest-looking commando force in history, but none was stranger looking than Maria Jane. She also had shed clothing, her skirt and cape were gone, so she now menaced the smugglers in plunging yellow bodice and lacy black drawers. Her wig was askew, but her gun was held with the fierceness of a mother whose child is threatened. Those mother-in-action hormones—no force on earth can resist. "Go ahead," Maria Jane said. "Make my day." The guard dropped his gun.

Immediately Maria Jane's face dissolved into a smug joy. "I've always wanted to say that," she said.

"Hope that courier or whatever didn't hear the gunfire," Sherry said.

"He did. Quick, we've got to make things look normal," Molly said, "or we'll never figure out what's going on. I've got an idea."

"She gets good ideas," Amanda said. "Listen up, everybody."

"All of you, get back down into the hole. Secure the prisoners down there." Molly looked around at everybody's garb. "Bently, Amanda, you're the only two who look the part, so you stay with me. Now go. Hurry."

Sherry looked at her father. He nodded. "I think I see her plan," he said. "I'll stay up here and hide in case she gets in trouble. Take everybody else through the tunnels to the house. Be easier to get a police transport to the house than to the campgrounds anyway." He pulled out his walkie-talkie to give instructions to his deputies.

"Don't forget the two that are tied up down there," Amanda said.

"Flo, I need to borrow this," Molly said, and took her scarf. Flo's eyes glared pure hatred, but she said nothing.

"Wonder how much this cost," Molly said to no one in particular as she took off the bandanna and tried to arrange the scarf in its place. "I'm out of practice. Been years since I've dressed for a city office. Don't know how to tie these anymore. Amanda, Bently, pretend to be unloading the wagon. I'll hold the horses."

"Those are Percherons, Molly. They're a mellow-tempered breed. Don't think you have to worry about them bolting," Matins said.

"Hide, you idiot. We don't know how close this so-called courier is."

Molly fussed with her scarf a little more, patted her hair, and tried to think herself into elegance. *If I pretend I'm well dressed, maybe this person won't notice I'm wearing Rebel rags. He'll think I'm Flo.* She examined the scarf. The design was woven, not printed, of cashmere and silk. *Flo sure has style,* she thought, and then recalled with a chill that she had thought Luke had style in assembling that bouquet. *Could it have been Flo who put together that bouquet? Could Flo have made the threats to Bonnie? Her own daughter? But why?*

Another crashing, followed by violent sneezing, announced the arrival of the courier. A small, balding man wearing a catalog's concept of outdoor wear approached now. Blue oxford shirt with maroon piping. Black string tie with turquoise clasp. Chinos with cargo pockets. Leather belt with silver-and-turquoise buckle. Loafers. *In short, nice clothes, an urban vision of Southwest style, but wrong for anyone actually wanting to walk in a woods. I thought hoopskirts were crazy enough in these* briars, Molly said to herself as she considered the loafers. He was not carrying a gun, she was glad to see, at least not in his hands.

"Not fair," the man said. "I jog every day. I thought I was ready for this hike, but nobody said you had hills."

"Well, this is hill county," Molly said. "I thought you knew that."

"How do you do," he said. "You must be Flo. They said look for the woman in the designer scarf."

"Yes," Molly said, hoping that he didn't expect to be greeted by name himself.

"What was the shooting for?"

"This eager beaver wanted to test one."

"Crazy. Don't you know the woods are crawling with people today? Some kind of social event. Where's Dwight?"

"He's down the hole already," Molly said.

"Is that all the help you have to unload the wagon?"

"For now."

"Well then, let's finish our business now. Too many people around for me. I'll not wait for the wagon as we'd planned. I'll walk out. The highway is that way?" He pointed east.

"Yes, and not far. Any other messages for me?" Molly said.

"Yes, the buyer will be here on Tuesday."

"What time?"

"I'm not sure."

"Wearing what?"

"How the hell would I know what she'd wear?"

She? Molly thought. "It would help me to know," she said.

"A dress, I guess. Who knows what women wear to tea? And what does it matter?"

"Matters a lot to a woman, mister," Matins said, once again rising from the brush, semiautomatic in hand as before.

"Who are you?" the man said.

"I'm your hardworking neighborhood sheriff. Hands up."

"Smooth," Molly said. "Couldn't have been smoother if we'd rehearsed it."

"Can we stop with these boxes now, Mom?" Amanda complained.

"Yes, dear, in fact we really do need to get you two to a wedding."

The man was still baffled. "You're not Sam?"

"No," Matins said, "who are you?"

He was silent.

"Well, you have the right to remain silent, I suppose. Nice tie," Matins said.

NINETEEN

BOUQUET

"Now what?" Molly said. Or rather started to say. She was interrupted by a volley of gunfire to the northeast and jumped about a foot at sound of it.

"Relax, Molly, that's just the reenactors," Matins said with a grin. "I told them"—he indicated the walkie-talkie—"they could go ahead with their show since everything looked wrapped up here."

"Are our muskets where we dropped them?" Bently said.

"I think so."

"They'd better be. They're expensive. Maybe four or five hundred dollars apiece," said Amanda.

"Spoken like a true accountant's daughter," Bently said. "I'm going to get back there to guard them until the others come to claim them. Are you letting them go as soon as the smugglers are taken to the county jail?"

"Yes, only tell them not to leave the area. I've called the ATF and FBI. They're driving down from Columbus to question everybody, but it's going to take them two hours to get here."

"The troops will probably be there before you are," Amanda said. "You'll get to play hero after all."

"Haven't you had enough heroics for one day?" Molly said.

"Yes." He smiled. He kissed Amanda, handed her his

Confederate coat and hat, pulled his Union kepi from a pocket, adjusted it to a jaunty angle, and saluted Matins.

"Yes, you are a handsome devil. Now git," Matins said.

"We've got to hurry and get changed, Mom," Amanda said. "C'mon. Through the tunnels will be fastest." She started down the ladder.

"You coming, John?" Molly said.

"No, I'm going to study these guns before the ATF impounds them."

"They're Russian," Molly said.

"Mom thinks Russian Mafia," Amanda added.

"I'd heard rumors Russian guns were getting into the country."

"More boxes are down in some of the side caves."

"How many?"

"I have no idea. You will tell me everything you find out later, right?" Molly said. Her head now was the only part of her sticking out of the hole.

"Yes, now you git, too. You've a daughter to marry off."

Amanda and Molly hurried through the kitchen, past Zenith and her daughter, who were busily assembling the buffet. "More people? Oh, it's you Molly, Amanda. Thank goodness. What is going on? We're working here on these sandwiches, just minding our own business, when, oh Lord, I say twenty people marched through with these guns, you wouldn't believe the guns, scared me half to death. Then the police came and carted some of them away. They took Flo. Bonnie's gone with her. I'm going to go, too, to help them, as soon as I finish setting up here. What is going on?"

"I really appreciate your staying under such circumstances, but we'll be okay. Go take care of your relations."

Zenith nodded and wiped her hands on her floral-print apron. "Zenith's Bridal Boutique" was emblazoned on the front. For a fleeting second Molly wondered if the apron did double duty as a greenhouse apron, then decided that was a completely unkind thought.

"Sherry told me to tell you not to worry about walking back to the cabin, that she'd send someone to get you," Zenith said.

"Who?"

"Well, she didn't say. Her exact words, in fact, were 'Tell them I'll send the cavalry to rescue them.' I assume that meant she's sending a cruiser. Anyway, I think you can probably take a little more time getting cleaned up for the ceremony."

"Thank goodness. That Sherry is amazing, always thinking. I'm going to take a shower, then," Molly said. "I need it."

As it turned out, Sherry wasn't kidding. It was the cavalry that arrived to take them to the cabin. The two Union riders in double-breasted frock coats, long leather gloves, and plumed hats, clattered from the woods and tied up to two horse stanchions on the kitchen porch. Until that exact second the stanchions had been mere ornaments to Molly. She now realized they had probably been put there for horses when the mansion was built. The two men stepped into the kitchen with a rattle of sabers, a jangle of spurs, and a creak of leather. Apparently their boots were new. Molly smiled to herself.

"Good afternoon, Mrs. West. My orders are to escort you and your daughter to the ceremony. If you will come with us," he said, taking her hand.

"How romantic," Amanda cooed.

Who was this daughter of hers? Molly thought. One moment she was coolly toting a submachine gun and the next she was adither over some male adorned with a phallic sym—a saber.

Amanda saw Molly's stormy face and laughed. "Just enjoy the moment, Mother. How often do you get to ride a horse in a hoopskirt?"

"I hope not ever again. What is your name, young man?"

"Lieutenant James Donegal," he said, removing his hat and bowing low.

"Any relation to Captain Donegal?"

"His devoted son. We have to hurry, ladies, the battle is almost at an end."

The men assisted the women to sidesaddle positions over the saddle horns, then climbed up behind them. Molly decided she had never in her life been more uncomfortable, and that included two pregnancies and births.

"Hang tight," Lieutenant Donegal said, and he spurred the horse into a trot.

Oh God, Molly thought, please, not a trot.

A bluish smoke rose over the clearing where the firing was. She saw "bodies" littering the field ahead and two double lines of soldiers facing each other, both standing, neither behind cover.

"They shot at"—gasp—"each other in the op—hhhhh—en like that? Those are authennnnnntic tactics?"

"Yes, ma'am, although later in the war there was some experimentation with hide-and-shoot tactics like we use today, but early on they used those outdated stand-up tactics with these almost modern weapons."

"No—won—der so—mmmmany died." She was

about to decide that conversation on horseback was not worth the effort.

"Most died from disease, not gunfire. Soldiers weren't very well trained at aiming then. Firing on both sides was so poor that it's said it took a man's weight in lead to kill a single enemy."

The two horses pulled up just at the edge of the clearing and waited. Bently's reserve then rushed into the clearing from the west flank. A group of Confederates wheeled toward the new threat and part of the main Union force then ran between the two halves and surrounded them.

"That's our cue," Donegal said. "Hyah," and the horses sprang into a full gallop circling the field. The spectators and some soldiers began cheering and clapping. Everyone knew the arrival of the bride signaled the end of the battle. They reined in before the cabin. Amanda jumped gracefully off her horse, her hoops and the wedding dress swirling in a splendid Victorian flourish, and she fell with an equally Victorian flourish into Bently's waiting arms. The crowd cheered.

Molly sort of halfway fell off her horse, her hoops swaying with a nonsplendid bungee effect. And where is the waiting clasp of my true love, she grumbled to herself. The crowd did not cheer, but at least they didn't laugh. Donegal steadied her.

A bugle blew. The bodies on the field "resurrected." The cornet band emerged from the cabin and played "When Johnny Comes Marching Home," then "Dixie," and finally "Taps." Then Mary-Mary's lone violin played Wagner's "Wedding March" from *Lohengrin*. A hush fell over the crowd, and Ken, still in his colorful coat, stepped from the cabin, took Amanda's arm and led her to where the chaplain was standing under a tree near the spectators' area. The soldiers and other costumed participants followed behind. Bently took his place to Amanda's right and the simple, timeless words of the vows were spoken.

Louella was suddenly at Molly's elbow. "Yer the bride's mama. Why ain'tcha cryin'?"

That was it for Molly. She was gone, sobbing like a girl, or at least like a Type A. "She's so pretty," Molly whimpered happily.

Mary-Mary's violin erupted into a joyful jig. The soldiers, blue and gray, quickly formed a double line, crossed bayonets or sabers, and the newlyweds ran under. The brass band took its turn with a joyful noise and Amanda tossed her bouquet. Sherry caught it, to Betty's squealed delight. And then it was over. Invited guests strolled to the mansion, others located their picnic baskets.

Matins had missed the ceremony, but he was at the buffet. "I am informed by Amanda that I made a sexist remark when I arrested that courier, and I do wish to apologize," he said.

"You did?"

"Apparently my remark about dress being important to women makes assumptions about women that were overgeneralized and thus offensive to women."

"Amanda said that?"

"Amanda said that."

"Well, I did not take offense. I mean we are all at an event where everyone is obsessed with clothes, so I gave it no thought."

"So my apology is accepted?"

"Yes, indeed. Are those guns counted and impounded?" she asked.

"That they are."

"Were there a lot?"

"Almost twelve hundred."

"Holy saints above."

"Holy saints above?"

"Victorian etiquette. A lady can't say 'Jesus H. Christ.' Are the Feds happy with us?"

"They're never happy."

"John, is there any agency whose services you respect or admire?"

Matins slowly chewed a bite of sandwich. He seemed to mentally scan the workings of every bureaucracy he had known. "I'm kinda impressed by Zenith's catering service here," he said finally.

"And how about the government, those sworn enemies of your sworn enemies, the private militias."

"Nah, they're all idiots. Thank God Sherry was on the scene, or we'd have had a bloodbath."

"She did have a little help, John," Molly said testily.

"Yes, Molly." His tone was almost serious now. "Don't think I don't know it. I will probably never hear the end of it from everyone who was a hero today. There's no hero worship like the hero who worships himself."

"I have to say I have a new respect for girl talk after today," Molly said. "Not only did it get us out of a tight spot at the cabin, it was the source of Louella's information."

"Yes, once again, Louella was right," Matins said.

"Louella was right about whut?" said Louella herself, coming up behind them.

"Hi, Louella. You were right about there being Farons and Wheelers involved," Molly said.

"Yeah, both Dwight and Sam Faron were in on it," said Matins.

"And Robert Wheeler, too?" asked Louella.

"No, Robert wasn't the Wheeler," Matins said.

"He waren't?"

"Nope, it was Flo." Matins laughed at her expression. "Well, Louella, I do believe that is the first time I've caught you in a surprise."

"Now I think on it, I see the sense of it." Louella recovered her composure in a hurry. "She be one troubled woman, has been since she ware a little thing."

THE BALL that evening was a rousing event, livelier than any wedding dance Molly had ever been to. The dancers whirled about the bonfires. Every Union soldier she'd rescued earlier asked her to waltz, each one hugged her and expressed "deepest gratitude" for her "fair valor."

Ken danced, too, clumsily attempting the waltz steps. "Face it," he said to Molly after countless kicks to her ankles, "we learned the Twist and the Frug." His dancing made her grateful for the sheathing of the hoopskirts.

"Let's sit," Molly said.

They settled on one of Zenith's borrowed straw bales and then burst into laughter.

"We both look ridiculous, don't we?" he said.

"Yes, but aren't we having fun? Except for that kidnapping, this has been a fantastic day," Molly said.

"We hadn't a clue, we just thought the delay was normal foul-ups, the hurry-up-and-wait syndrome of most human social events."

"Ken, don't you dare play sociologist. Don't you dare analyze this. I'm enjoying this. I don't want to think. I think this is the first wedding in my life that is any fun. I don't want to know why."

"Me too. Except for ours," Ken said.

"Including ours. My dad got drunk. Your mom scolded him, which made my mom mad. Your sister fell and twisted her ankle. My cousin backed her car out a driveway and hit a passing motorist. It was a zoo."

"I don't remember any of that. All I remember is how beautiful you looked."

"I was fat. I was pregnant, remember?"

"You are even more beautiful now."

"I'm even more fat now."

"Such a grouchy lady. Why do I love her?"

"Because she makes you such nice clothes?"

"I was the envy of the Confederacy. No one had ever seen anything more authentic. To be able to say this coat was based on a real diary, everyone was so jealous. Can you dance again?"

"Oh no. These shoes are killing me. How could those women stand it?"

"Maybe they hurt just because they're new. New shoes hurt in any century."

She laughed.

He took her hand tenderly. "So sit with me on the hay, my love, and—"

"Straw."

"Straw, sit with me on the straw, my love, and let us together thank God, the sheriff, and his talented daughter that you and Amanda didn't get your fool heads blown off today."

"You know, I think Sherry's new undercover work is with the militia groups."

"Molly, don't you dare play semiofficial temporary deputy. Don't you dare analyze this."

She was silent. After a minute he said, "Okay, okay,

I can't stand it. Why do you think Sherry's working on militia groups?''

''She just knew too much today. She knew how the federal agencies think; she knew the guns; she seemed to know how the militiamen think. You were right, too, you know.''

''Me?''

''You said we should be looking for criminals, not militia types.''

''Maybe John will make me an official semitemporary deputy, too. At twice the pay, of course.''

''You'd have to swear not to lecture to the felons.''

''I don't lecture. I just talk with substance.''

''You know, I should ask John to pay me for my work.''

''Thing I can't figure,'' Ken said, ''is why today? The risk of doing something like that delivery with so many people about—that just seems to me beyond stupid.''

''Oh, I figured that out the minute I saw that wagon,'' Molly said. ''They planned all along to come out through here, through the campgrounds. They'd come in by the lightly used logging trails, but come out by driving that empty wagon right by everybody. No one would think anything of it. Everyone was expecting the wagon. Even if it were spotted before it was unloaded, people would think it was just on its way to the reenactment.''

''I still think a quiet day would make more sense.''

''No. If they came in on a quiet day, a forester might spot them and wonder what they were doing. Or if they used a logging truck instead of the wagon, sure, you'd expect to see a logging truck in a managed forest, but, still, a forester might want to see their permits. No, it was real clever of them to use a public event as cover. No one—cop, forester, civilian—would stop them to investigate that wagon. I wonder now, how many times have I seen that wagon at some public event over the years, how many of those times had it just come from a pickup or a delivery?''

"Then what went wrong?"

"I think their big mistake was trying to play militia. If that picket hadn't been so gung ho, if he'd stayed hidden as he was probably told to, none of us would have known about the delivery at all."

"Makes sense. Maybe John *should* pay you."

"Mind if I join you two lovebirds for a minute?" They turned. Matins. Molly scooted aside and he sat beside her. "Hay bale's not quite big enough for three, is it?" he said.

"Straw," Ken said.

"I know the difference, damn it. I'll sit on the ground. No, I'll lie on the ground and try to get rid of this headache."

"Having a bad night?"

"Oh yes. No one's talking. The Feds couldn't question a ten-year-old. I've just come from the jail. If they'd let me talk to Flo, I'm sure I could get her story, but no. They're the smart ones; they've been trained, you see." He scowled. "Poor Bonnie. I told her she might as well come to the ball. Her mother will probably be in jail all night. She's so upset, poor kid."

"She there now?"

"Yeah."

"Why'd you leave?"

"Gotta dance with my women, or they won't speak to me for a month."

"You're not in costume."

"Molly, this hillbilly shirt was native garb at least a generation before the War Between the States. Only the hat is wrong. Let me borrow your slouch hat, Ken, so I can appease the love of my life and her lovely, pistol-packing daughter with a waltz or two.''

"I know what the Feds are doing wrong without my even being there to see. They're asking her direct questions, aren't they?'' Molly said.

"Yeah, so Flo's insisting she was just with her boyfriend, Samuel, that she was practically their prisoner, that she had no idea those were guns in that little ol' wagon, and what could we be thinking of to think that a nice lady like her, et cetera, et cetera.''

"And Sam?''

"He's pretending he's a prisoner of war and only has to give his name and rank.''

"Dwight, the others?''

"Same. They're my people, why can't they let me take care of this? I know how to talk to 'em.''

"And that stranger, that courier?''

"He's a gangster out of Las Vegas.''

"Las Vegas?''

"Isn't that bizarre?'' Matins said.

"Outsiders. Why can't people go home and leave us alone?'' Ken said.

Matins smiled at him and shook his head. "Yeah,'' Matins said. "Compared to them, you guys are natives. Especially if I could get the ATF out of our hair, we could break this whole chain. Arresting Sam, Flo, and her friends will interrupt the flow of guns a little, maybe push it out of the Tricounty at least, but with big-time Mafia behind this, until we know where the guns are going, we aren't going to stop them. Those guns may bypass the Tricounty now, but they are going to get into the cities to kill people like my Sherry.''

"Flo's the key, isn't she?'' Molly said.

"Why do you say so?"

"Well, I was thinking earlier today how much style she has. She has too much money for a woman who doesn't work and has no husband and is the daughter of a bankrupt store owner. I was thinking that whoever sent threats to Bonnie sure had a lot of style. I was thinking that a body in the middle of a smuggling center was just too much of a coincidence not to be relevant, and I was thinking what you said Ken, way back last February, when this started."

"What was that?"

"All violence is family violence, you said."

Both Ken and the sheriff nodded slowly.

TWENTY

TEA

EMPTY LIKE THIS the mansion seemed haunted. Ghosts of Bartons seemed to sit on the faded chairs and sofas. Bonnie was at work. Flo was still in jail. Molly, with ever-deepening misgivings, was at the mansion waiting for the gun buyer. It was early Tuesday morning and all she could think of was how much could go wrong: what if someone had warned the buyer away, what if the tea wasn't supposed to be at the mansion at all, what if the buyer showed up with a semi wanting to load before negotiating, what if she showed up with armed henchmen?

"Molly, Sherry and I will be hidden right by you," Matins said. "We'll put a wire on you so we can hear everything you say and you'll wear a bulletproof vest. If you need another person in the room, Sherry can pretend to be Bonnie. If she needs to inspect the goods, we've put two in the kitchen on top one of the Hoosiers."

The plan was for Molly to converse with the buyer while Sherry and John listened. Both Tricounty patrol cars were hidden nearby as well, one in the woods, one below the driveway. Matins was nervous about the plan, too, but not for the same reasons as Molly. "I can't keep the ATF at bay much longer. Either this trap of mine with the buyer has to work on Tuesday, or all those clowns will come in and with them media, media, media.

The Tricounty will become another Montana or Texas. So, Molly, will you help, will you pretend to be Flo?''

"Maybe the ATF has learned from its mistakes. Maybe you can trust them not to foul up,'' she protested.

"How much cold cash you willing to bet on that?''

"Why do you need me?''

"You're about the same age as Flo, about her size, even.''

"Ken will kill *me* if I get killed.''

"Cheer up, the commissioners will kill me if you get killed. I never wanted to ask you to do anything dangerous. The only reason I'm asking now is this is a perfect chance to crack this thing for good. I don't know who else to ask. If whoever is coming doesn't know Flo, you'll be able to talk to her for a while, maybe find out some things. And if she does know Flo, well, at least we get her in the house, which should be enough to show cause to question her.''

Flo was still in jail awaiting her arraignment and bond hearing, mainly because Matins had called in a favor or two. He didn't want Flo out and able to talk to her contacts for a few days. So at his request Judge Gains had a sudden stomachache on Monday, forcing a delay in the process until, oh, maybe Wednesday at the earliest. A very bad stomach, very bad indeed. According to Matins, Flo hadn't budged from her story that she was just a kidnap victim. She was used. Guns? What guns? How dare they put her in jail, and her a God-fearing, taxpaying woman.

"So please, Molly. Judge Gains says his stomach has to get well by Wednesday morning. The ATF says I can try my idea once, and then I'm out of the game. I need you.''

"When is this woman expected?''

"Who knows? Our overdressed courier didn't say and won't say anything more. Naturally, he won't say anything more. The FBI are doing the questioning."

"Are you allowed to say such awful things about the FBI?"

"Yeah. It's written into my contract."

"I thought you were elected."

"Are you or aren't you going to help me?"

"Does the FBI know you're using a civilian to help you?"

"I told them I was using a deputy. That's the truth almost, you know. You did swear to be an official semi-temporary deputy. You did; I was there."

"I must have been out of my mind."

So Molly, feeling four times fatter in her bulletproof vest than she ever did in her hoopskirt, had a whole day to kill. They were keeping the tea water hot and the tea service ready all day, but Molly figured "tea" really meant "high tea." And high tea, Flo would know given her heritage, meant four in the afternoon with tea accompanied by pastries. At first Molly felt too shy to poke and probe, but the house was just too interesting not to let her curiosity run free. She explored at will and haphazardly through every room and cabinet.

In the kitchen she found a collection of painted tins in one cupboard, which delighted her. She loved collectibles like that. Most of the tins had things like rubber bands, paper clips, or cookie cutters in them. But several held herbal tea blends. One tin in particular caught her interest. It was a beautiful, square, dark green tin with vines painted on it in black and gold. On the bottom a crude X was painted in nail polish. She sniffed the contents and wrinkled her nose. Smelled like dried compost, she thought. In another cupboard she found a good supply of baking ingredients and decided to pass the time by baking a linzer torte for the tea.

Matins and Sherry were also exploring the contents of the house, but their search was more systematic, more professional. They went through each room, picking up each item, carefully putting it back exactly where they found it. Matins had complained at Sherry's insisting on such tidy searching, but Sherry had explained, "Dad, we don't know who else uses this house. Some other smuggler may visit and notice something out of place. Let's assume the mansion is real important in this operation and make sure we don't scare anybody away until we know more."

Matins had smiled admiringly at his daughter. "I see why you got that promotion."

Molly could hear their conversation from time to time, and once they talked about Sherry's undercover work.

"Is there anything you can tell me about it?" John said.

"Just that you were right, we're trying to infiltrate some paramilitary groups."

"It was Molly who guessed that. There are groups in Columbus?"

"Oh sure. They're as active in cities as they are in rural areas. One of the biggest in the country is in New York."

"Do you think we're facing a real armed revolt in this country?"

"I doubt it. The more I see of it, the more I think they're just men who weren't very popular as kids looking for a way to feel special. Too bad innocent people have to die for these goons to feel special."

"They're guys who couldn't get girls?"

"That's a tad overspoken, but they are men, and some

women, too, who need to imagine somebody is against them in order to feel life has any purpose.''

"No communists anymore, the only enemy left is the government.''

"And blacks, Jews, Hispanics, Asians. And Northerners if you're Southern, Southerners if you're Northern, Easterners if you're Western, and everybody hates Californians.''

"Every one of these militia types I've ever talked to had a bad family situation growing up,'' John said. "Dr. K always says all violence is family violence.''

"Really, I never looked at it that way before,'' Sherry said, "but maybe so. They're unhappy people looking for something to blame for their misery, something, anything, other than themselves.''

"Are they dangerous?''

"Some are for sure, but most are just sad, so sad. I've started to pity them,'' Sherry said.

"Pity will get you killed, gal. Pity is the ultimate insult for a man.''

"I know.''

The two eventually finished their search and joined Molly in the kitchen. She set out a lunch of leftovers from Saturday's buffet, which they ate in silence. The day dragged on and boredom set in. John began reading *Godey's Lady's Books*. Sherry began dusting the china in the dining room. Molly decided to inspect Flo's clothes closet. If she were going to play Flo, she should dress like her, she decided.

Molly pulled on the light cord and studied the garments. What is this closet telling me? she thought. Hanging with each dress or suit were accessories in a Ziploc bag. Each bag was attached to the hanger by a clothespin. Shoes were lined up on a rack, each with its mate, each with some paper stuffed in the toe to protect the shape. She sure loved her clothes, maybe more than her house, Molly thought. As a girl, she must have been able to have any clothes she wanted from her father's department store. Wonder if she ever forgave him for going bankrupt?

The room was neat, the opposite of the overdecorated parlors below. The only untidy thing in the room was a stack of child's drawings, most signed, "I love you Mommie, Bonnie." Which is Flo? Molly wondered, Type A or Type B? A woman caught in an abusive marriage, the child of a remote mother and a failed father, might kill if she were Type B, she might indeed. Molly selected the blue dress Flo had worn to Amanda's February brunch. It was a little snug because of the vest, but not uncomfortably so. She spun around, inspecting the fit in a mirror. Flo sure has style, she thought yet again.

And still the day dragged on. Molly began fluffing cushions in the parlors. In the second parlor she paused in mid-fluff and remembered Lorraine DeWitt's comment about the furniture. Her interior decorator's eye had noticed an unnatural grouping of chairs. Why would a neatnik like Flo set her chairs this way?

"John, help me shift these chairs," Molly said.

"C'mon, Molly. Sherry said don't disturb anything and I think she's right."

"No, there's something odd about these. Let's inspect."

When the chair's skirts had cleared the spot, they saw a small trapdoor. Inside a box built between the joists were a gold necklace, several pairs of diamond earrings, two cashbooks and a huge volume of cash.

Matins whistled at sight of the money. "Sherry, count

the cash. Molly, you're the accountant. What do you think all this means?''

She inspected the cashbooks. ''The dates go back seven years.''

''Seven, not six?'' John said.

''Yeah, a year before David's disappearance, the same year as Bonnie's marriage,'' Molly said.

''Very interesting.''

''Is the handwriting Flo's?'' Molly said.

''I can't remember her hand on her statements, but it's possible,'' Matins said.

''My guess is these are account books for the gun smuggling. No matter what the business, you need account books,'' Molly said.

''There's forty thousand here,'' Sherry said. ''Maybe it was intended to pay for the delivery on Saturday, the one we interrupted,'' she added.

''Is Flo a risk capitalist then?'' Molly said with a strange tone in her voice.

''A what?''

''Someone who puts money up front, before she's sold the goods.''

''What do you mean?''

''If she's the middleman she can double or triple her money,'' Molly said. ''If she's only passing the goods along, the most she can charge is a percentage, sort of a rental fee for the caves. But if instead she pays for the goods and resells them, she could double or triple her money. My respect for Flo has just doubled, maybe tripled.''

''Okay, Molly, I'm only an underpaid sheriff. Explain that again.''

Molly smiled. ''We have the Chinese to thank for inventing the hundred percent markup way back in some dynasty or other. Doubling the price from wholesale to retail is fairly normal in legal commerce and has been for umpteen thousand years, so let's assume tripling it may be the norm in illegal commerce. But commerce is commerce. Buy low. Sell high.''

''So this forty thousand is what?''

''The low. That's a crucial piece of information for us. If this tea this afternoon is really a negotiation, knowing that forty thousand is the low gives me a number to work with. That may be all I need to pull off this Flo act. I feel like I can do it now, I know what the stakes are. Oh-oh, I smell my torte, I need to check the oven. John, be careful with those magazines, they're priceless. Sherry, pick me some flowers from the yard. Dollar amounts that high require a certain flair in the negotiating chamber.''

John and Sherry exchanged a shrug. ''Why do I get the feeling that I am no longer the senior officer in this case?'' John said.

''Is she always this bossy?'' Sherry asked with a soft smile.

''I heard that,'' Molly said, but she was thinking, Am I where Amanda gets her bossiness from? No. Never. Not a possibility.

As she pulled the torte from the oven she had another thought. ''John, exactly how many guns were delivered Saturday?''

''I don't know; I just counted them all together.''

''Damn, it sure would help to know the going price per gun.'' She put the torte on a rack to cool and called Ken at his campus office. ''I need you to surf the Net for me.''

''The Web?''

''Whatever. Find me either the retail or wholesale price of a Russian semiautomatic.''

"Good God. Molly, where are you and what are you doing?"

"Don't call me; I'll call you. Is twenty minutes enough time? It'll be three-thirty then, plenty of time."

"Time for what?"

"I love you. Bye," she said.

THE NEWS isn't good," Ken said when she called him back.

"You couldn't find it?"

"Oh sure, found it on the first try."

"So, tell me."

"Molly, the Web sites for Russian gun manufacturers are in Russian."

"Oh."

"I did check out the Web pages for a few other manufacturers, and you're not going to like what I found."

"Tell me anyway."

"Prices ranged from a low of $123 for a Chinese gun to $26,000 for a hand-tooled American. Pretty useless. I'm sorry, love. Best I can do so quickly."

"No, Ken, no information is useless, I've decided. I might not be talking to you if you hadn't learned—from the Web no less—that twigs can be used for crochet. I'll make sense of this somehow." She thought a while, then decided to assume $123 was the lowest retail anywhere, but that the usual going price for a quality gun was probably the four or five hundred that Amanda and Bently paid for their reproduction muskets.

Precisely at 3:55 p.m. Molly set out the tea service in the front parlor. Sherry placed the flower vase, then disappeared. John squeezed into a cabinet in the doorway between the two parlors, less than ten feet from where Molly sat.

"Pray I don't sneeze," he said.

Precisely at 4:02, a Lincoln Town Car pulled into the drive and parked in front of the portico. Probably rented at the Columbus airport, Molly thought. Columbus was the nearest commercial airport, almost a seventy-mile drive from this house.

A woman in an expensive tweed suit stepped out. She carried a black patent purse that matched her shoes and she carried a small gift-wrapped parcel in her hand. The hostess gift, of course. Molly was immediately grateful for all the time she'd spent getting ready for the reenactment. Before the wedding she was just an ex-Chicago suburban girl whose idea of elegance was an outdoor barbecue with matching paper plates and napkins. But for the reenactment she had learned Victorian etiquette, including tea protocols. The hostess always pours, the hostess always pours, she repeated to herself, suddenly very nervous. She was sure she could pull off the financial knowledge Flo must have had as the daughter of a store owner, but she wasn't sure she could also pretend to be descended from faded wealth.

She's descended from a pirate, Louella would say. Molly imagined Louella scolding her as the doorbell rang. Thank you, Louella, she breathed. Just thinking of Louella's hard-boiled style toughed her. She opened the door with a broad smile.

"Mrs. Wheeler?" the woman said.

"Yes, of course, please come in."

"How do you do," she said, removing a glove and extending her hand. "I'm Edna Faron." Molly's eyebrows flew up at that, but she quickly controlled her face. The woman most certainly was not Samuel's mother, the Edna Faron who had helped with Amanda's veil, the Edna Faron whose slip in conversation had almost given away too much. Maybe this was an agreed-upon code name. How many little traps like this lay ahead in this conversation?

"How kind of you to come," Molly said, slipping into the Victorian syntax Amanda had taught her.

"I have so wanted to meet you, Mrs. Wheeler. You have many admirers in the city."

"Are things well in the city?" What city, what city, please say what city, she thought.

The woman laughed. "If you believe the papers, crime is down, pollution is down, commerce is up. It's a fine place to live."

"Are you happy there?"

"Oh yes. If you can afford it, it's a wonderful place. I wouldn't want to be poor there, however. I stopped at a restaurant on the drive down. Prices are so unbelievably low down here."

"We have a comfortable life." How much time should she spend on small talk? Molly worried to herself. Who should initiate the negotiation? She knew how to talk to a woman; she just didn't know how to talk to a woman criminal. Well, maybe girl talk is girl talk, no matter what the women do for a living. Now if the woman across from her were an Appalachian she'd know what to do. No direct questions, tell a story, wait for a better story. It would be so simple. But what did this woman expect from a conversation? Well, the best strategy must be to act like Flo. Flo was an Appalachian. Flo would be indirect, and Flo would never mention money even if the topic of the conversation were money.

"Try this torte. It's fresh," Molly said.

"Thank you. This is a marvelous house."

"It was built in the 1840s by the first Clement Barton, a river entrepreneur."

The woman smiled. "Entrepreneur indeed."

"Would you like to see a little of it? I have samples of the goods in the kitchen. That'll give me a chance to show you some of the things we have. Everything you see has been in the family, some of it since the early 1800s."

Molly continued this way and, thanks to Amanda's tour, was able to answer every one of the woman's questions about objects that caught her eye. In the kitchen the woman spotted the cupboards. "Oh my, I haven't seen a Hoosier cabinet since I was a girl, and here you have two."

"The samples are on top of that one," Molly pointed. The woman stretched, took one down, disassembled and then reassembled it competently and smoothly. Molly struggled to contain her surprise. "Very nice," the woman said. "Much better than I was expecting. You hear such stories about the shoddiness of Russian goods, but these will do very nicely."

The woman replaced the guns on top of the Hoosier. "Oh, I love that huge hearth. You do have a treasure in this house. Is the family planning to restore it?"

"We can't decide. I suppose it would be wisest to sell it to a historical association and go live someplace else," Molly said.

"I'm considering Brazil myself," the woman said.

"Oh, have you been there?" Molly said.

The woman looked at her, suddenly suspicious. "Of course I have."

Molly hastily tried to recover the woman's trust. "I wasn't sure if you went personally, I mean. But of course, it would make sense for you to go." So the guns come from Russia, through Brazil, to the Southwest to Ohio, but then to where?

"You're right, though. The truth is, I only went on recreational trips until my husband's heart attack. Now that he's gone, I'm going to try to manage the business myself."

"We were so sorry to hear about his death." In a way, Molly was sincere. How much information died with whoever he was?

"I'll admit I didn't know how I would feel about meeting you. I do miss him. I loved that gangster. I can understand why you were his mistress."

Molly was grateful the teacup was in front of her face at that second. "He was a wonderful man," she choked out somehow.

"One couldn't help loving him. I knew he loved me, too, even if... But it was his admiration for you, for your business skill, that is helping me to try to go on myself. I have you to thank for my courage today. This is my first time negotiating on my own. I confess to being a bit nervous."

You're nervous? Molly thought. So was Flo sleeping with both Sam and what's his name? Was she carrying on before David was killed? What a tangle this clothes-obsessed woman was.

"Shall we commence, then?" Molly said.

"I'm prepared to offer you one," the woman said.

One what? Molly thought. One hundred thousand for the 1,200 guns? Not bad, especially for an opening. Or one hundred per gun? Also, not bad. With the high cost of living in wherever she was from, one hundred might seem logical for a low bid. Molly had expected fifty as the opening, either fifty thousand or fifty dollars per gun.

"Oh, I had been led to expect five," Molly cooed as she cut two more slices of the torte. She thought she heard a gasp from John in the closet.

"Five is steep. The only way we could consider it is if you handle shipping and delivery."

"No, we're simply not equipped for that." Boy, was that the truth, Molly thought. "Perhaps we could split the difference at three-fifty."

"Done then. My husband always acted like this was so difficult, but here we are agreed in seconds."

"I think it's that we are women. Women are so practical, don't you think?" Molly said.

"May I have some more of that tea? It's very good. Unusual flavor."

"My sister-in-law blends them. They are very popular locally."

"I shall have to buy some to take back to New York."

New York? Oh my word, I've been negotiating with a New Yorker? Molly thought. If I'd known that, I couldn't have done it. But she seems so nice, maybe she's not a native New Yorker. "I'll be glad to give you samples. Was your flight from the city comfortable?"

"Oh yes. My son came with me. I left him in Columbus visiting OSU. He's thinking about going there next year. I want him to stay in the city, maybe NYU or Columbia, but I think he wants to get away from home."

"I can understand that. Bonnie has been tense since she's had to move back home. I know she wants her own place."

"Doesn't her being home cause problems with the business?"

"Yes, you're very perceptive. It's been difficult. I want to give her a trailer, but how would I explain to her how I can afford it."

"I see your problem. I'll tell you something awful. When I heard about Bonnie's poisoning, I thought it was like David again. We always wondered how David disappeared and never an inquiry. It was poison, wasn't it? But why poison Bonnie? Is her living in the mansion that much of a risk?''

Molly flopped back in her chair, too shocked to speak. She couldn't think of anything to say. She could play Flo no longer. "John," she said. "John, help me."

John stepped from his closet.

"Howdy, ma'am. Whoever you are, you have the right to remain silent. You have the right to an attorney. If you cannot afford an attorney, we'll git you one, y'heah?"

"Dad," said Sherry as she came into the parlor, "that's not quite right."

"Well, hell, I don't get to say it all that often. There's not all that much crime in the Tricounty."

The woman stood, her mouth slack, her eyes brimming with tears. "How could you?" she said. "How could you do this to me, Zenith?"

TWENTY-ONE

DISHES

"I CAN'T BELIEVE she thinks I'm Zenith," said Molly.

"I can't believe you don't know your Miranda text, Dad," said Sherry.

"I can't believe I just willingly did the cop-in-the-closet thing," said Matins.

The three sat in the kitchen nibbling leftovers again, the excellent deli leftovers catered by a possible poisoner, Molly thought. Only in Appalachia could a poisoner also be a professional caterer.

None had recovered from surprise yet. Matins had sent one deputy to take the woman to the county jail and had sent the other to pick up Zenith for questioning. But he wasn't ready to leave himself to face the FBI and ATF yet. He didn't have his theory together; he didn't want to walk in the county building and report to those arrogant, full-of-themselves smugasses until he had all the answers. He had his pride to consider.

"What's wrong with the cop-in-the-closet bit?" Molly asked.

"Just not my style. Too all-fired corny."

Molly thought, is this the same man whose idea of dressed up is a plaid shirt for a jacket? But then if the reenactment had taught her anything, it was that style values were both extremely personal and often intensely felt. People could care about appearances too much. The fanatic stitch counter was a common ego type not only at reenactments, but in any work or hobby, from copy-editing to paramilitarism. Watching the costumed dancers at the ball, she'd concluded everyone has a little stitch counter inside them.

"Well," Matins said, rubbing his throbbing facial muscles. "Back to Square One. What do we know and when did we know it?"

"Thought One," said Molly falling into her listmaker mode, "'Zenith' could be a code name just as 'Edna Faron' is that woman's code name."

"It's not her code name," said Sherry. "There really was a minor gangster named Tony Faron who died of a heart attack last year. And his widow is named Edna."

"How'd you know that?"

"It was in the Columbus papers. The couple funds a scholarship at OSU."

"See? No one's completely evil," said Molly.

"Oh, but he was," said Sherry. "I think he used the OSU link as an excuse to come to Ohio frequently. We knew he had something going here, but we didn't know what, and we thought it had died with him."

"Okay, so could Zenith really be the mastermind here, the one who runs it, and Flo be just as she claims, just a go-along, Sam's little helpmate?" said John.

"If so, why didn't Zenith warn Edna away?" Sherry said.

"Maybe she didn't know who the buyer was now that Tony was dead or that she was coming. Remember, the courier's message was given only to Molly. And we've worked hard to keep Flo from talking to anybody," said John.

"Or maybe Zenith's hoping the whole thing will be pinned on Flo," said Molly.

"Maybe. A little thin, though," said John. Sherry nodded.

"Wonder how the whole thing got started?" said Molly.

"Well, I can put together a nice good-ol'-boy scenario," John said. "Let's say Tony Faron comes into Ohio about seven, eight years ago, isn't that about the time legal semiautomatics got really scarce, Sherry?"

She nodded.

"So he comes in looking for new transport routes and he knows, hell, everybody in the world knows paramilitary types are thick as ticks in May down here. Doesn't take him long to find Sam or find out that Sam has access to big trucks."

"And a team and wagon," said Molly.

"I bet that wagon idea came later. Anyway, they get to talking, find out that Sam's mother and Tony's wife have the same name."

"Hell of a coincidence, that," Sherry said.

"I don't think so," said Molly. "Faron's a common name anywhere, and Edna was common once, sort of the Jennifer of sixty years ago. Read the obituaries. An Edna dies almost every week."

"Yeah, it's a real plausible coincidence," said Matins. "For Sam that's all he needs to trust Tony. A good omen like that is irresistible to a good ol' boy. Meanwhile Sam meets Flo, gets tangled—"

"Oh, I bet the Flo and Sam thing goes back further than that. You forget how pretty Flo was when she was young," Sherry said.

"How would they meet up?" Molly said.

"Molly, this is the Tricounty. Everybody knows everybody," John said.

"No, I bet I know how they hooked up," Sherry said.

"Dwight's a little older than Amy; he might have been in school with Bonnie. Parents always meet the parents of other kids. They see each other on sports nights, parents' nights, bus-route hearings."

"Yes, that's it," Molly said. "I never knew how political bus routes could be until I lived in a rural area. Everybody goes to those. And what Sherry says is true. We know more people through our kids than we've ever known through church or work."

"Okay," John continued his scenario, "so they meet, they take up together. When this business opportunity comes along, Flo with her brains and business savvy was handy."

"So why call in Zenith?" said Sherry.

"Capital," Molly said. Both frowned at her in puzzlement.

"I was wondering how Flo got her up-front money. I remembered Amanda kept complaining about missing pieces of furniture when she showed me the house, so I assumed Flo must have sold off some pieces for capital, but it couldn't yield enough, not if most deals were over a quarter million like today. She probably talked to Zenith, who has several million dollars in assets, much of it in equity even, but like all businesses, she must be cash poor. Zenith might have negotiated some paper for Flo in exchange for ready cash."

"I don't follow."

"I mean, I doubt she would have taken out a conventional and easily audited mortgage. But she might have put some deeds up as collateral for some early transactions. In the process, the two women might have discovered they worked well together, and a partnership was forged."

"I agree," John said. "Flo and Zenith are probably

equal partners in this. As sisters-in-law they're close enough emotionally. Both have enough business skills. And bluntly, both are smart enough, much smarter than either of their husbands. But, like our friend Edna, I can't figure why poison Bonnie. David, sure. If Flo and Zenith made this thing work by sleeping with the key men, Flo with Sam and Zenith with this Tony, then David would have been a nuisance. His jealousy, his violence—sure, get rid of him. Robert is passive, bland, stupid, no need to kill him. David is another matter. But why Bonnie?''

"I do not believe Flo poisoned her own daughter,'' Molly said.

"Why so?''

"They're just too tightly bonded.''

"You said they quarrel a lot,'' Matins said.

"Yes, but they're the quarrels of love. Amanda and I are the same. We fight all the time. We don't throw dishes like Flo and Bonnie do, but we fuss. We fuss because we love each other. I want to protect Amanda from pain. She wants me to be perfect, someone she can always admire.''

"A lot of mothers and daughters are like that,'' Sherry said, obviously thinking of her own mother. "Maybe that's why daughters are more at ease with their fathers.''

"Or the reverse; if their fathers abuse their mothers, it's why they may hate their fathers so intensely,'' Molly said.

"What are you saying?'' Matins said.

"The only messy thing in Flo's bedroom upstairs is her collection of Bonnie's girlhood drawings. Her daughter is the most important love of her life. And Bonnie's love for Flo matches it.''

"It's a dysfunctional love, then,'' Sherry said.

"It's a dysfunctional world,'' Matins said.

"But what if Luke were the target of the poisoning—" Molly began.

"Well, the mother wanting to protect her daughter would certainly make sense then, except for one detail. I don't think Flo or Zenith are stupid enough to try a poisoning with three cops in the house," Matins said.

"But maybe protection wasn't the motive," Molly said.

"What?"

"Let's think about this from a different direction," Molly said. "Remember when the accounts started."

"Yeah, about a year before David disappeared. So maybe it took a year before he got to be a big nuisance."

"No, it was also the year Bonnie got married, the year she would have left this house."

"Molly, I don't follow at all."

"Bonnie wouldn't have known why the furniture was disappearing. She might have thought it was David who was selling it, not her mom. If Zenith is the poisoner, she has no reason to poison anybody—David, Luke, or Bonnie. If Flo is the poisoner, she has reason to poison only David. But if Bonnie is the poisoner, then everything makes sense."

"You think Bonnie is in on this gun business?"

"No. She probably never knew about it. Flo and Zenith are for sure smugglers, but they're not murderers."

"You really think it's Bon—"

The door opened. Bonnie. Home from work. "Oh? What? Hello?" She was confused, surprised to see them sitting there.

"Hi, Bonnie, we've been helping ourselves to these leftovers here," Molly said.

"And trying to finish this investigation," John said. "I'm afraid we have bad news for you. We think we have enough to build a case against your mom and now your aunt, too, for smuggling. But we have good news, too—we are pretty sure they didn't murder your father. So at most they'll get five to six years."

"Oh, honey, you've had such a terrible time lately," Molly said. "Here, sit down. I'll fix you some tea."

"Thank you." Her hands were trembling.

"We're working on the theory right now that someone in Sam's gang got a little eager and killed him," John said, tugging his lip. Molly used to think that gesture meant "I'm thinking," but now she was starting to think it meant "I'm lying." "Truth is," he continued, "we have no idea who did it. Is there anything you can tell us, now that you know a local paramilitary group was involved in this smuggling thing?"

Bonnie shook her head. Molly handed her the cup. She warmed her hands on it for a few seconds, then sipped slowly. She took several sips as the others sat in silence.

"One thing I'll say about your Aunt Zenith's teas is they're so restorative," Molly said. "One sip of one and I feel I can do anything. I found tins and tins of the teas in your cupboards here. I don't know what they are, but I know they're all going to be good. I made the one you're drinking from this tin here." Molly set the dark green tin, the one with the red X on the bottom, in front of Bonnie. Instantly Bonnie jumped from her chair, shaking in panic.

"So you know that tin holds poison, don't you, Bonnie?" Molly said. "I thought you'd know. That's the tea you meant to give Luke that night and somehow you drank it instead. You sent those threats to yourself, didn't you? I noticed the scrawl on them is like the printing on your girlhood drawings in your mother's room."

Bonnie clutched the back of the chair. "Mom said Luke would get his revenge," she said.

"Yes," Molly said. "Luke knew you'd killed your father. With him feeling penitent, he was dangerous. With him wanting to atone for his sins, he was sure to confess to someone he'd helped you."

"Why did you kill your father?" Matins said very softly.

"This tea works really fast," Bonnie pleaded. "Please, get me to the hospital."

"Tell me why you killed him, then I'll call."

"He was destroying everything in this house, the things in it, my heritage. He'd sell it or throw it or break it. Every time he'd get mad he'd break something priceless."

"You made the poster and the bouquet yourself," Sherry said. "But where did you get that toy gun?"

"I'd had it already. Luke loved guns, so I got him the toy as a gag gift, a stocking stuffer for Christmas once."

"John, all you need is a deputy, not an ambulance. I didn't give her that tea," Molly said.

"I know that, Molly. You take me for an idjit? I've already punched for Briggs. He's on his way."

"Okay, Molly, give us the rest of it," Sherry said. "What made you suspect Bonnie?"

"Oh, lots of things. Her Civil War enthusiasm means she had to know most of the stories I heard from the Tricounty Old Ladies Network, including—now whose story was it?—right, Katrin Wilton-Jones's story about the Virginia poisoner, the man who tried to poison his bride, but poisoned himself instead. I thought she could have gotten the idea to poison Luke by switching cups with him."

"Sherry, you were in the kitchen with them," John said. "Do you remember anything?"

"I know Bonnie made the tea, but, wait, I do remember something. Flo put the creamer and sugar bowl on the tray, but to do it, she turned the tray around rather than reach over the teacups."

"That classical upbringing again. A lady doesn't reach over things. But in so doing she reversed the cups. You think Bonnie didn't see her spin the tray?" Molly said.

"Probably not. Luke was so intense that night. Now that I think on it, perhaps he did plan to try to persuade her to confess, to not live with her 'sin' anymore."

"So she might not have seen her mother spin the tray?" John said.

Sherry nodded.

"Then she could have handed him the cup in front of her, planning when he fell to tell people that the cup was intended for her, just like in the story, not knowing her mother had already switched the cups," Molly said.

"Okay, that explains how she might have botched the attempt to poison Luke," John said, "but why did you begin to suspect her of murdering her father?"

"Maybe you have to be a mother to understand these things. Her reaction when Flo smashed a saucer was extreme. I felt more was going on between them than a message about dishes. When Amanda showed me the house the very next day, I noticed all the mismatched dishes in the dining room, as if a lot had been broken. I wondered if a violent man had done most of the breaking. Amanda had told me many times she worried about Bonnie's low self-esteem from her father's or Luke's beatings. Ken says low self-esteem is a major cause of violence. I noticed Bonnie's mood swings several times myself. At the reenactment Bonnie had the most beautifully made dress of any woman there. I wondered at the time if she were a stitch counter, a fanatic who takes it too seriously. Almost everyone at the reenactment complained about these fanatics, although no one would actually admit to being one."

"That's true," Sherry said. "It was always someone else who was the fanatic. One of the soldiers at the ball explained it to me this way. He said, 'Authentics are what we do, farbs are people who cut corners more than we do, and stitch counters are people who cut corners less than we do.'"

"Right after Bonnie married," Molly continued, "expensive things start disappearing from this house. She assumes her father is selling them, not her mother, mainly because her father has broken or damaged so much already. Reenacting is all she has, it's her identity. He's destroying her, she thinks. That might have been enough. Fanatics can do extreme things. And one does not have to be a paramilitarist to be a fanatic with low self-esteem."

"Why'd she tell us about the body, do you think?" John said.

"Remember how uncomfortable she was around Dawn? She had to know about the February pilgrimages to the most famous Underground Railroad site in the Tricounty. The church group could find the body at any moment, maybe that very morning. When she saw the body had resurfaced, she was afraid she had no time to move it or rebury it. Maybe she believed if she told us about it herself first, it would deflect suspicion."

"How'd she get the tea?" John said.

"Every teenager in the Tricounty has worked for Zenith at one time or another. Bonnie probably mixed it herself at the greenhouse six years ago and it's been in the cupboard ever since.''

"If you're right, Bonnie probably wrote that note saying David left for another woman?''

"Maybe.''

"How'd she get David to walk down into the caves?'' John said.

"That one's tougher to figure,'' Molly said. "Maybe the poison was fresher then; it might have been slower acting, giving her time to ask him to come down to look at something.''

Bonnie had been listening to all this in silence.

"No, he fell in the kitchen,'' Bonnie said, never lifting her gaze from the table. "He'd been beating Mom, again. He wanted money. I thought that meant he was going to sell something again. I made the tea to try to calm him down. I'd had it for months, but couldn't get the nerve to use it. It wasn't just the things he broke or sold. It was Mom. She always tried to protect me. But I couldn't protect her from him. Listening to their screaming that night—it was too much. No more. He fell here.'' She pointed to a spot in front of the hearth. "Mom, Luke, and I took him down while he was still warm. We never tied him. It was just easier to bury him folded up like that. I wrote that note, yes, but it was Luke and Mom's idea. Yes, I poisoned Dad, but I had help to bury him. But you're wrong about Mom. It was Dad selling that furniture. Not Mom.''

"Are you sure, Bonnie?'' Molly said as gently as she could. "She did need money to finance her gunrunning.''

Bonnie looked into her cup. "This tea is safe?''

"Yes.''

"More, please. I'm not sure of anything right now. I never knew about the guns, the smuggling. No wonder she didn't want me back in the house. Mom sell those things? Maybe. Mom never felt about this house like I did. I don't know. I don't know anything anymore.''

Deputy Briggs had arrived for Bonnie. "How many more Wheeler women do you have up your sleeve?" he whispered to Matins.

"Show a little respect," Matins growled. "This is a sad, sad family, a sad, sad house. You'll lock up before you leave, Molly?" John said.

"Yes, I just want to return this dress to Flo's closet first.''

"It's a pretty blue," Sherry said, turning in the doorway. "How would you describe it? Royal blue? Azure blue?"

"No, I think—'' She hesitated, pondering Sherry's question with some seriousness. And pondering, too, how would she comfort Amanda when she learned her childhood friend was a murderess. How would Amanda react? With denial, seeing Bonnie as victim? With betrayal, feeling she'd given her friendship to someone in error? Would she judge the choices of a child with the values of an adult and blame herself? Or would she blame her mother for destroying her friend? Molly had willingly helped with the investigation, after all.

How does one mother an adult daughter? The rich, delicious smell of the season's first honeysuckle floated in through the doorway. Honeysuckle was a hated weed, a vine that strangled and smothered all other plants, like a mother who mothers too much. Yet its orchid-shaped flowers and lush scent, dense as fog, were sweeter than all other wildflowers, like a mother's love, too. The blue of this dress was as paradoxical as that, as the honeysuckle, as a mother—so beautiful, so aggressively beautiful and yet so desperately sad. "I think I'd describe it as 'something blue,'" she said, "just 'something blue.'"

AFTERWORD

ALL THE CIVIL WAR stories in the text are based on true stories. An infant really was stolen from a Kentucky overseer's bedroom. A Virginian really tried to poison his bride. A New Orleans diarist really sewed coats from oilcloth tablecovers. Some of the stories come from John Beatty's memoirs, who while in no way connected to anyone in the fictional Tricounty, of course, was a real general, and he wrote a spectacular diary. It was first published as *The Citizen Soldier* in 1879 and was republished by Norton in 1946 as *Memoirs of a Volunteer.* Another excellent source of contemporary Civil War detail is *Hardtack and Coffee: The Unwritten Story of Army Life* by John D. Billings, first published by Smith & Co. in 1887, but later reprinted in 1982 as one of the volumes in the Time-Life Collector's Library of the Civil War.

Dawn's tales about the fictional Zachariah Williams are loosely based on the autobiography of John Parker— *His Promised Land,* edited by Stuart Seely Sprague (Norton, 1996). Parker was a freed slave who owned a foundry in Ripley, Ohio, and conducted some spectacular forays into Kentucky to bring out slaves.

Tales of Morgan's Raiders, including those of Lightning Ellsworth and the one of the desperate galloping battle between George Eastin and Colonel Haisley are from Dee Alexander Brown's *Morgan's Raiders* (Smithmark, 1959).

The Civil War may have been the first war in history where many of the combatants were literate, so there are thousands of diaries, memoirs, collected letters, and regimental histories. The Ohio University Archives has a sizable Civil War collection from families in this area which I used extensively.

Many details about reenactors and reenacting came from *Reliving the Civil War: A Reenactor's Handbook* by R. Lee Hadden (Stackpole Books, 1996) and the *Civil War Supply Catalogue* by Alan Wellikoff (Crown, 1996).

But the best source of both Civil War lore and reenacting customs came from reenactors themselves, and I especially want to thank members of the Ohio 91st, who host the wonderful Buffington Island reenactment every year in late July. It's a great party. Y'all ought to come. For information, contact the Meigs County Historical Association, P.O. Box 145, Pomeroy, Ohio 45769.

—Patricia Westfall
June 1997

A DOUBLE COFFIN

GWENDOLINE BUTLER

A COMMANDER JOHN COFFIN MYSTERY

Former British Prime Minister Richard Lavender still knows when things need handling quickly and discreetly. Lavender's father was a serial killer. And the ex-PM wants to put matters right, nearly three-quarters of a century later. Hence the summons to Commander John Coffin of London's Second City police.

But when a journalist investigating Lavender is murdered, past and present collide, proving what Coffin already knows: that the past never disappears—it's buried, only to resurface in shocking and menacing ways.

Available May 1999 at your favorite retail outlet.

FIXED
in his
FOLLY

David J. Walker

A MALACHY FOLEY MYSTERY

When high-powered attorney Harriet Mallory develops maternal instincts for the child she gave up for adoption thirty-one years ago, it's Mal Foley's reputation for discretion that lands him in her plush ofice.

But when he locates Harriet's son, now an alcoholic priest on a downward spiral, Foley discovers a man trapped in a maelstrom of vengeance and death. Threats targeting all of the priest's "family, friends and fools" are being systematically carried out. Foley's not sure if he's a friend or a fool, but he just may be the next to die.

Avaiable July 1999 at your favorite retail outlet.

A CULINARY MYSTERY

The table is set, the wine is breathing and the television viewers are invited to delight in Darina Lisle's next episode of her top-rated food series, *Table for Four*. Death isn't on the menu until Darina's charming costar, Australian wine expert Bruce Bennett, drops dead on camera.

Has one of the other guests poisoned the brash Aussie? Darina starts from scratch, and unless she unmasks a killer before the plot thickens, she might become the final ingredient in a recipe for how to create the perfect murder.

Available July 1999 at your favorite retail outlet.

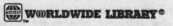